W9-AVC-558

DEC   2012

CHASING THE SKIP

JANCI PATTERSON

CHASING THE SKIP

Christy Ottaviano Books

HENRY HOLT AND COMPANY

NEW YORK

Henry Holt and Company, LLC
Publishers since 1866
175 Fifth Avenue
New York, New York 10010
macteenbooks.com

Library of Congress Cataloging-in-Publication Data
Patterson, Janci.
Chasing the skip / Janci Patterson.
p. cm.
"Christy Ottaviano Books."
Summary: When fifteen-year-old Ricki's mother finally leaves for good,
Ricki's absentee father steps in, taking Ricki with him as he chases bail "skips"
across the country, but their fledgling relationship is tested as they pursue attractive,
manipulative seventeen-year-old Ian Burnham.
ISBN 978-0-8050-9391-9 (hardback)
ISBN 978-0-8050-9637-8 (e-book)
[1. Fathers and daughters—Fiction. 2. Fugitives from justice—
Fiction. 3. Bounty hunters—Fiction. 4. Automobile travel—Fiction.] I. Title.
PZ7.P276535Ch 2012 [Fic] 2012006164

First Edition—2012/Designed by April Ward

Printed in the United States of America by
R. R. Donnelley & Sons Company, Harrisonburg, Virginia

1 3 5 7 9 10 8 6 4 2

For Drew, who believed in me
enough to tie his future to mine

CHASING THE SKIP

I-25 outside Thornton, Colorado.
Days since Mom left: 29.
Distance from Salt Lake City, Utah: 530.67 miles.

1

I sat in the passenger seat of Dad's four-door truck, trying to focus on my history assignment and not on the skip sitting behind me. I'd watched Dad cuff her hands—discreetly, so as not to make a scene. He'd chained the cuffs to a bolt in the floor to keep her from reaching up, and then chained her feet as well. I'd never been this close to a fugitive before, and I kept expecting her to break free and jump onto the freeway, even though she hadn't resisted when Dad chained her in.

The skip's name was Alison, and I wasn't supposed to talk to her. Dad said too much talking made him seem soft and the distraction made it easier for skips to escape. But the twenty-minute ride back to Denver was too long for me to keep my mouth shut.

Alison leaned over the back of my seat. She looked four or five years older than me, which would make her nineteen or twenty. If I ran into her on the street, I wouldn't have thought anything of it. In her cami and tight-tight jeans, she didn't look like she was running from the law.

Dad had frisked her when he picked her up, and thrown a bag of weed into a Dumpster. Doing her a favor, he called it. She didn't seem out of it, so she probably wasn't on anything now.

"How did you find me?" Alison asked.

Dad leaned his head back on his headrest. "I sent you a letter at your last address," he said.

Alison's face was only a few inches from mine. Her lips were chapped, like she'd been chewing them.

"I didn't get any letter," she said.

Dad smiled. "No, you didn't. But the post office did. They were kind enough to write your new address on it and send it back to me."

"Oh," Alison said.

I opened my notebook on top of my history text. On the first blank page I jotted down the date, Alison's name, and the name of the freeway. I like to keep track of details like that—things I see, things I do.

"Yeah," Dad said. "Next time you jump bail, you might try leaving your mail behind."

I'd made Dad reset the odometer when he picked me up. Dad had driven 745.23 miles since then. I wrote that number down beside Alison's name.

I tilted the cover of my history book so Dad wouldn't see what I was writing. *Dad found Alison through postal return,* I wrote. *If you're running from the law, forget about your mail.* That trick seemed pretty clever to me. Dad probably hadn't thought it up himself. I'd have to write about it in my blog when I could get to a computer. My best friend, Anna, was always thinking up ways to spy on people. She'd love to know how a professional did it.

"I didn't realize anyone would come after me," Alison said.

"Most people don't."

Alison sat back, chain clinking against the floor bolt. Even though Dad hadn't said so, I figured the chain on her hands was to keep her from strangling me with the cuffs.

"Besides," Dad said, "you were staying with your cousin. I'd have gotten around to looking there eventually."

"I should have thought of that. I guess I didn't think I was in that kind of trouble."

"Bail bond enforcement is serious business. If I hadn't come looking for you, someone else would have."

3

"Bail bond enforcement" is the PC term for bounty hunting. I guess the more direct term must freak people out, because Dad told me not to use it except with him.

When I was little, Mom told me that being a bounty hunter meant Dad was out fighting crime. There was so much crime in the world that he just didn't have time to take me home with him and be a father. When other girls were playing with Barbie dolls, I was wearing a cape and leaping around the house, fighting imaginary crime with my imaginary dad. I used to think I'd grow up and be a hero with him, and then we could be a family.

The first time I remember seeing Dad, I was eight. He came through town looking for a skip and stopped to pick me up. I packed a bag with my binoculars and my jump rope, which I thought we could use to tie the skip up when we found him. Instead, Dad took me to McDonald's and tried to get me to play on its playground. He didn't say much—just asked me about school. When he dropped me off, I threw the binoculars out the window of our third-floor apartment. So much for adventure.

When I was ten, I realized that fighting crime was actually pretty dangerous. I used to tell myself that Dad didn't come by much because he was protecting me. If the people he chased knew he had a daughter, they'd kidnap me and hold me for ransom. And in my daydreams,

I'd fight my way out and help Dad catch them. When he saw how useful I could be, he'd want to pick me up and take me along.

Around the time I turned thirteen, I stopped pretending and Mom stopped telling me stories. Dad wasn't around because he chose not to be. Mom wasn't stopping him from picking me up for the weekend, but he rarely bothered. They'd separated before I was even born, so we'd never been a family. I got my last name from him, but that's all I could expect to get. I told myself that was okay. Mom was right: Life gave you what it gave you, and what I got was a Dad who didn't care. I didn't need him. But sometimes when I was bored in class I'd think about him. Did the thrill of the hunt make up for the loss of his daughter?

And then, last year, he started calling once a month. Could he drop by to see me? Could he take me for the weekend? He'd really like to talk.

Mom would wave the phone at me whenever he called, talking loudly at me so he'd know I was home. But I always got off the phone as quick as I could. Leave it to my deadbeat Dad to start caring just when I'd decided not to anymore.

And now here I was, living my childhood dream. But the first skip he took me along to find was Alison, a skinny girl almost my age who had failed to pay child support. Some crime-fighting life. Some reason to ditch your daughter.

I glanced back at Alison. She caught me looking at her and half smiled, which made me feel like I should say something.

"It must be humiliating to be chained up like that," I said.

"Ricki," Dad said in a warning tone. I pretended I hadn't heard him.

"Did you really not support your kid?" I asked. She looked too young to have children.

Alison sighed. "It's complicated."

Dad shook his head. "You got a child, right?"

"Yeah."

"I don't see what's so complicated about it, then," Dad said. "If you've got kids, you support them."

"You living my life?" Alison asked.

"Thankfully, no," Dad said.

"Then mind your own business."

Dad watched the road in front of him. "Pretty soon your business will be between you and the judge."

Alison didn't respond. I wished she would. It was nice to hear someone besides me arguing with Dad.

I turned back to my list, writing down the reason for Alison's arrest. Mom said Dad always paid his support right on time, every month. Still, there was more to being a parent than money.

"You studying?" Dad asked me.

"I'm taking notes," I said. Which was true, they just weren't the kind he was thinking of.

"Good girl."

I wanted to write down how condescending Dad was being, but I didn't. Instead I sat with my pen hovering over the paper, bouncing up and down with the grain of the road. When I made lists, I tried to keep them objective. Ms. Nielson, my journalism teacher, said reporters always write down the facts and details, trying not to make judgments about anything. I liked that idea. I captured the world the way it was. Like a photo. Some of my friends from school wrote angsty lyrics about how miserable their lives were, but what did that get them? Tears, a runny nose, and a reputation for drama.

I pressed the ballpoint to my notepad, deciding on some words. *Dad thinks if you have a kid, you should pay child support. Paying for them is the law, but spending time with them isn't.*

When we pulled into the parking lot of the county jail, Dad removed Alison's chains and let her walk in uncuffed. She hadn't been any trouble when he picked her up, so I guess he wasn't worried about her running away. Plus, Dad was a big guy. He could take her down if he had to.

Alison's shoulders hunched like she'd just gotten home from a very long walk. Dad stood straight and tall. He was dressed in jeans and a blue button-up shirt. His undershirt had this weird swoop neck, so his chest hair poked out right below his collar. He kept his hair cut above his ears—not long or dreadlocked. He didn't wear chains or leather or have obvious tattoos. But despite his lame clothes, he managed to pull off a commanding presence through posture alone. I couldn't help but be impressed.

Dad held the door open for Alison, like he was some kind of gentleman instead of her bounty hunter, and they disappeared inside. I wondered if Alison would end up in prison. It didn't seem right that Dad had ignored me for most of fifteen years and now here he was bringing her in like some kind of hero.

I lifted my pen to the page. *Dad walks with his shoulders thrown back, so he swaggers like a sheriff in a western.* I smiled. That would have to go in the blog too. My boyfriend, Jamie, would love it. He liked to watch this show on cable called *Big Mike: Bounty Hunter.* Big Mike was always getting pumped up chasing after murderers and getting in gunfights. Ever since I told Jamie that's what my father did for a living, he'd been bugging me for details about my TV dad. I hated to disappoint him, but my dad was nothing like Big Mike.

I thumbed through the first pages of my notebook, to

8

the spot where Jamie had stolen it and written in it himself, right below my tally of how many times Mr. Brandt had said "more or less" during our geology lesson. Final tally: thirty-two.

In the margin, Jamie had drawn a picture of Mr. Brandt with his eyes crossed, flipping me off.

Jamie always made fun of me for my lists. I didn't get what the big deal was. It's not any weirder than the emo poetry in my school's lit journal.

I hadn't gotten to talk to Jamie since Dad picked me up last week. I checked the dash to see if Dad had left his phone behind so I could call Jamie's cell, but he hadn't.

When Dad opened the truck door, I jumped. He climbed in and slammed the door.

"So that's it?" I asked.

"What do you mean?"

"I mean that's all you have to do? Pack up the skips and take them to a jail?"

"Sounds easier than it is sometimes. I've got to get them to a jail in the county where they were arrested. The farther they run, the farther I have to drag them back."

"Why can't you just turn them in to the cops?"

"I don't get paid unless I take them in myself. Sometimes the cops beat me to it, but on the small jobs, usually not."

I'd seen that on TV. Big Mike got really pissed whenever the cops beat him to an arrest. He always had to psych himself up with an extra-big job to get over it.

"I need to go see Cal," Dad said. "Just got off the phone with him. He's got another job for me."

"Maybe we could go back to Grandma's first? To see if Mom's there?" Grandma lived in Salt Lake, which was an eight-hour drive from Denver, and an hour from Mom's old place. Jamie didn't have money for gas, so I hadn't seen him since the night Mom disappeared and I took the bus up to Grandma's. At least then we'd been able to talk on my cell phone, before it got shut off.

Mom often left for a week or so without notice, and I'd catch a bus to stay with Grandma until she came back. Grandma always said that Mom shouldn't be abandoning me just to take trips with her boyfriends. She'd glare and huff when Mom came to pick me up, but we all knew she didn't want me staying alone, either.

But this time Mom had been gone for a month. Three weeks in, Grandma decided she couldn't deal with me anymore, so she convinced Dad to come pick me up. A month was a long time to go without school, or seeing Anna or Jamie. Or Mom, for that matter. I should have just crashed with Anna instead of going to Grandma's. Anna wouldn't have called my dad. Her parents would have been nosy about it, though.

"I called your grandmother, too," Dad said. "She still hasn't heard anything."

"But maybe Mom will show up while we're on our way there. She's never been gone this long before."

Dad shook his head. "Grandma will call me as soon as she hears from your mom. I'll drive you back when that happens."

"Even if you're in the middle of a job?"

"Even then."

Dad started up the truck and backed out onto the street. Silence stretched between us, and I tried to think of something else to talk about. On the drive from Salt Lake to Denver I'd thought I'd punish him by not talking at all. Then I realized he actually *likes* the silence. I guess you'd have to if you were going to drive all over the country by yourself chasing skips—the only company Dad seemed to need were his recorded books. Besides, after three weeks with no one but Grandma to talk to and then a week stuck in Dad's parked travel trailer, all I wanted to do was talk.

"How old is Alison?" I asked.

"Twenty-one."

"She looks younger than that."

"Yeah, well, she acts pretty young too."

"What's that supposed to mean?"

Dad sighed. "It means she doesn't take responsibility

for her own life. And her own kid. I pick up a lot of people like that."

"People who don't pay child support?"

"People who don't take responsibility for their choices."

"Being young isn't the same as being irresponsible."

"Sometimes it is."

"I'm younger than her, and I'm responsible." Mom always told me that. I did most of the cooking, and a lot of the shopping. I'd had a credit card in her name and a fake ID that said I was her since I was thirteen, so I could buy food when she forgot.

Dad looked over at me, but he didn't respond.

"You don't think so?"

"You getting that homework done?"

I rolled my eyes. "I'm responsible for things that matter."

"Homework does matter."

"It's not like you're Mr. Education. You just did bail enforcement training in a couple of states."

"Maybe I want better for you."

"Whatever."

"Besides, not all education comes from school." He patted the music player on the dashboard. "I may be on the road, but I'm always learning something. I can download audio versions of your English books, if that'll make it easier for you. Maybe you're an auditory learner like me."

"Maybe not," I said. "I think I'm more of a hands-on person."

"Yeah," Dad said. "Your mom was like that too."

"See?" I said. "I'm not being irresponsible. I just take after her."

"I suppose she's proof of your point. Responsibility doesn't come with age, after all."

I gritted my teeth. "Don't talk about her like that."

Dad's chin dropped slightly, and he was quiet for a moment.

"I'm sorry," he said. "You're right. I shouldn't say things like that in front of you."

"Maybe you shouldn't say things like that *at all*."

"Sorry."

"Whatever. Why are you apologizing to me?" Mom never did, so I wasn't sure how to respond.

"Because I feel bad for what I said. Responsible people apologize when they upset someone."

"Thank you, Mr. Rogers."

Dad laughed then, which also wasn't the response I expected.

What stung was that I knew he was right about Mom. She worked to support us, of course, although she counted on me to do a lot of the responsible stuff other moms did for their kids. But she was a single mom, which was harder. Besides, it wasn't like I didn't get anything out of the deal.

I never had a curfew. Mom would let me leave whenever I wanted and come home when I pleased. And a couple of times a week she didn't even come home at night herself. She said that's why I was more responsible: She didn't give me anything to rebel against.

I pulled out my notebook again, opening to the page where I left off. *Dad and I are headed out to find him another job. Mom still hasn't called.* Maybe if I put that last part in the blog, Mom would see it and call me.

"At least you're getting some homework done now," Dad said. "I'm glad I brought you along today."

I smiled.

"And I don't think you're irresponsible. You just need to apply some of that responsibility to your education."

"Yeah," I said. "I get it."

If Mom could run off, leaving her job and our apartment and all her other responsibilities, I didn't see why I should keep being the responsible one. Look where all that responsibility got me. Stuck on the road with a father who'd never wanted me and a mother who'd disappeared for a month. The way I saw it, life was easier for irresponsible people.

2

alvin Zabrinsky owned a bail bond office in downtown Denver. I expected it to be in a seedy neighborhood surrounded by liquor stores, pawn shops, and payday loan places. Instead the office sat in a sleek building with glass walls, right between a psychiatrist and a law firm.

Dad parked the truck so that it faced the shopping center across the street. When he opened the truck door, the cold October wind slapped me in the face. I unbuckled my seat belt, but Dad shook his head.

"Wait here," he said. "This won't take long."

I sighed as Dad disappeared into the building. A girl could only take so much waiting, so I followed him. Dad wouldn't complain once I got in there—not in front of Cal, anyway.

I checked my watch. Three o'clock. If Mom hadn't disappeared, I'd be riding on the back of Jamie's motorcycle, headed home from school. What would Jamie be doing without me? He'd better not be giving a ride to some other girl. I'd have to e-mail Anna later, to ask her to check up on him.

I took my time walking across the parking lot to Cal's office. As I opened the door, a little bell rang over my head. Dad stood across a counter from a football-shaped man. His body sloped to a point at his head and feet, with a big, round belly in between.

Dad already had his check in hand. Both he and Cal looked at me. They glanced at each other, and then Cal cleared his throat. They were probably talking about me.

"You must be Ricki," Cal said, a fake-chipper tone to his voice. "I was just asking Max when he was going to bring you in."

I was glad Dad had the sense to go by Max, which was the first part of Maxwell, our last name. Max was a much better bounty-hunter name than Robert, his real first name. Of course, Cal knew both of Dad's names.

"Well, here I am," I said, looking at Dad. "Are you done?"

Dad shook his head. "Take a seat." He turned back to Cal. "How about that other job?"

Cal watched Dad for a second, as if he was trying to

decide something. "Okay," he said. "Just a second." He disappeared back into his office. Dad took a lollipop out of the basket on the counter and waved it at me. "You want one?" he asked.

"No, thanks. Mom says you are what you eat."

"Candy?" Dad asked.

"A sucker."

Dad smiled. "I walked into that one."

I plopped myself down in a seat and picked up a copy of *Time* magazine. I was behind on the news, but so is *Time*, since it only comes out once a week. I wondered if Cal's clients were really that interested in politics. Maybe if *Time* did a lot of articles about prison reform.

The cover story in this issue was about a bombing in Afghanistan. The cover had a picture of the secretary of state standing right next to the Afghan leader, deep in conversation. That story broke while I was at Grandma's, reading the news on her ultraslow Internet.

Cal came back and handed a folder to Dad, who looked the papers over.

"It's what you asked for," Cal said.

"You take requests?" I asked.

Cal laughed. "Not exactly."

Dad chewed at the corner of his mouth.

"What's the matter?" Cal asked. "Not what you wanted?"

"No," Dad said. "It's fine."

"What's the problem?" I asked.

Dad flipped another page. "Nothing."

Cal shrugged. "It's a little riskier than usual, is all."

"Riskier?" I asked Dad. "What kind of danger are you putting me in?"

Dad shook his head at me, and I returned the sweetest smile I could manage.

"Really, Max," Cal said, "if you're not sure, you don't have to take it. Could be rough with your daughter along."

Dad shook his head. "We'll manage."

Cal rolled his eyes. "I should have gone with my gut and steered clear of this one. I knew he was going to run, but he's a kid. I've got a soft spot for kids."

"He's seventeen," Dad said, looking at the paperwork. "That's old enough to know better."

That was even younger than Alison. "Don't you ever go after adults?" I asked.

Dad didn't look back at me. "Sure," he said. "Just have a couple of young ones this week, that's all."

"It's my fault," Cal said. "I'm the one taking the risk on 'em. You can have a different job, if you want. I've got a guy who skipped on reckless driving. Pay's not as good, but it'd probably be quick."

"No," Dad said. "I'll take this one. He's just a kid, like you said."

Cal waved a finger at Dad. "I never said 'just.' 'Just' is a dangerous word for a bounty hunter."

"Bail bond enforcement officer," I said. Both Cal and Dad laughed.

Ms. Nielson said that journalists didn't just report the news. They asked deep questions to find the story. If Dad was hunting a kid, there had to be a story there somewhere.

"So who is this kid?" I asked.

"His name's Ian Burnham," Dad said. "Like the woods, but spelled differently."

I set the magazine back on the table. "The woods?"

Dad sighed, shaking his head at me. "We've got to get you listening to some Shakespeare, Rick."

"Don't call me Rick. That's a boy's name."

"Ricki's a boy's name too," Dad said. "But your mom sure liked it. She only named you Erica because your grandma insisted."

"Well, I like Ricki, not Rick. Are you done yet?"

"Almost," Dad said, looking over the papers. "This lists all the charges?"

"Just the ones they thought they could make stick."

Dad tapped his pen on the counter, squinting.

I stood up and walked over to the counter to grab that lollipop after all. If Dad was going to take this long about it, I needed sugar. "Do you think about all your jobs this much?"

"It pays to think twice," Dad said. Then he set the folder down on the counter and signed the top paper.

Cal took it from him, looked it over, and then signed it himself. He frowned at me. "You be careful, okay?" he said to Dad. "It could mean both our asses if she gets hurt."

"I'll take care of her," Dad said. "It'll just be a few more days."

In a few days I'd probably be back with Mom. I hoped Dad was right about that.

Cal opened his mouth like he was going to say something else but thought better of it. He opened a file drawer and dropped the signed paper into it.

Dad gave Cal a sharp nod, and we left. On our way across the parking lot, Dad shook his head at me.

"I'll drop you by the library for an hour. You need to get those homework assignments typed up and sent off."

I hadn't done any homework, but I kept my mouth shut about that. "I could do it tomorrow."

"I've got a meeting tonight, so you can do it now. I'll pick up dinner on my way back. What do you want?"

In the last week, we'd exhausted the range of fast food. "Tacos?" I said. At least those weren't deep fried.

"Tacos it is."

"What's this meeting? You already talked to Cal."

Dad was quiet for a second. "It's personal."

I sighed. "Fine." Maybe Dad had a girlfriend he didn't want me to know about. It's not like that would bother me. I didn't have any illusions about my parents getting back together. Mom had plenty of boyfriends.

Maybe his girlfriend didn't like kids or didn't know he had a daughter. I might be the one he was hiding, not her.

I steered the conversation back toward the job. "Why did Cal keep telling you that you don't have to take this one?"

"He worries. He's not comfortable with me taking you along. That's why I asked you to stay in the car."

"Whatever. Was he this concerned about Alison?"

"I don't think he expected Alison to be dangerous."

"I thought it was your job to bring in dangerous people." We reached the truck, and I walked around to the passenger side, still waiting for Dad to answer. We both climbed in.

"I don't usually take the riskier jobs," Dad said. "Ten little jobs will pay the bills just as well as one big one, and they're a lot safer besides."

"How would you know which ones are big ones?"

"More serious crimes. Longer sentences. People skipping child support or running from a drunk and disorderly aren't likely to shoot the guy who's coming to get them. A guy who's looking at prison for ten to fifteen, though . . ."

"So this kid. What's he looking at?"

Dad started the truck. "Nothing I can't handle," he said. "You just ride along and it'll be over before you know it."

The reporter questions were failing me. Then again, lots of people didn't want to talk to the press. Sometimes you had to find the right angle to get people to talk. "So my own dad doesn't care about my safety?"

Dad laughed. "You're good at this, you know."

"At what?"

"Asking sneaky questions to get what you want. You might be good at my job."

"Does that mean I can help you?"

"Oh, no. If I thought I couldn't keep you safe, I wouldn't take you with me. But that doesn't mean you're my new trainee."

It was worth the try. "So if you didn't think you could keep me safe, what would you do with me, then?"

"I'd figure something out."

"Yeah, well, like you said, it's only for a few more days. Mom will be back soon."

Dad sighed like he wanted to say something else bad about Mom, but he didn't.

After Dad dropped me off at the library, I got a code to use the library computer, but I didn't even touch my school website. The homeschool system was actually pretty cool—the assignments were all straight out of textbooks, so students could work them out on paper ahead of time and then fill out the online forms to send them in to be graded. Maybe if they'd offered journalism, I would have paid more attention to it, but of course they only had boring subjects like English and history and math.

I logged on to one of the public computers and pulled up my e-mail, jittering my knee up and down, up and down.

No new messages. Granted, it had only been yesterday that I last checked, but still. Jamie hadn't sent me one single e-mail since I'd left town. I knew he preferred texting, but it wasn't my fault Mom didn't pay the cell bill before she left. We'd just switched carriers, so I didn't know the password to go in and pay it myself.

It had only been a week since my phone got turned off, but a week was a long time for Jamie to ignore me. He could have bothered to write me an e-mail just this once. I'd already sent him several. I knew I shouldn't sound too needy, but sometimes weird things happened to e-mails— they got swallowed by cyberspace or whatever. Maybe he thought *I* was the one not e-mailing *him*.

Jamie Boy, I wrote.

Still haven't heard from you. Such a shame, since I'm off having fabulous adventures with my bounty hunter dad. Check the blog for details. E-mail me and I'll tell you all the stuff that doesn't go into the blog.
Ricki

I hesitated for a moment, trying to decide if I should sign the e-mail "Erica." Jamie always called me by my full name, ever since someone heard our names and thought I was Jamie and he was Ricky. In the end I left it. I liked Ricki better anyway.

What I really needed was a way Jamie could call me. I reached into my pocket, finding Dad's business card. Robert Maxwell. Bail Bond Enforcement. The card had his number on it, and an address for a P.O. box in Denver. He'd given me the card in case I needed to call him from the library or something. He'd just passed it across the seat like he was handing it to a client. He didn't ask why I didn't already have his phone number. He'd given it to me over the phone six times in the last year, but I'd lived fifteen years without it, so I never wrote it down. I was glad Dad didn't call me on that now.

I opened up a new e-mail, typed in the phone number and a quick message, and then sent it to my contacts list.

If Dad wasn't going to take me back to my friends, I could at least give them a way to call me. Anna would call, even if no one else did.

I leaned back, tipping my chair onto its hind legs, and pulled up my blog. Ms. Nielson said that you didn't have to work for a newspaper to be a journalist—people who blog report on what's happening around them. She said some of the most important journalism happened that way. Even in places like the Middle East, protests and political movements spread online through social media more than they did through the formal press. Even the journalists at the top newspapers read blogs to keep up on what was happening in the world. I didn't need good grades or anything to be a blogger. The blog I had now was for practice—when I got older I'd do a real one. I'd have lots of time to get good at it, and then when I had to support myself I could be one of those people making a living off their online writing.

I'd put pressure on this entry, though. It had to be fun and exciting so that Jamie and Anna would leave comments to find out more. That would be tough to do with unbiased details.

I've been with My Father, the Bounty Hunter, for a week now, though I just rode along with him for the first time today, like I was his partner. Big Mike

has several partners, but Dad just has me. He usually takes small jobs, but now he's taking on a big one, probably because he has me along to help.

I tapped my nails on the keyboard. Objectivity had abandoned me today. Dad wasn't treating me anything like a partner. Better get back to the facts. I opened my notebook to find some of the lists of details I'd made.

Dad's glove compartment is full of tools—binoculars, a Maglite, spare handcuffs, and a length of chain. He keeps his guns in the utility boxes on the sides of his pickup.

I hadn't actually seen the guns, but Dad said they were there.

His clipboard, phone, and GPS are Velcroed to the dash for quick access while he drives. We haven't gotten in any car chases yet. I'll take detailed notes when we do.

Did real journalists have a hard time making the truth sound exciting? The real story wasn't in the contents of Dad's truck; it was with the people he picked up. I paused, figuring out how to refer to Alison without putting in her name. I figured I could get Dad in trouble for that.

Instead I described Dad's arrest, calling Alison "the skip" and paying special attention to the part where he backed her against the door frame and yelled, "You're under arrest!"

When I was finished, I ran a search for *Ethan Frome*. I'd only been in the homeschool program a week, and I already had a book report past due. I scanned through a few summaries of the book before clicking over to the *New York Times* to read about the peace negotiations between Palestine and Israel.

When the computer logged me off for going overtime, I let the chair legs fall back to the floor with a thud. I'd been here over an hour. Time to go meet Dad.

Denver, Colorado.
Days since Mom left: 29.
Distance from Salt Lake City, Utah: 539.23 miles.

3

Dad was waiting in the parking lot. I climbed into the truck and unwrapped a taco, filling my mouth with cheese and shell.

"You could wait until we get home," Dad said. "We could set the table, even."

"I'm hungry," I said, talking through a mouthful of taco to illustrate my point. "And that trailer is not a home."

Dad sighed, but he didn't argue.

As we pulled into the RV park in Sheridan, rain splattered across the windshield. I'd downed all three of my tacos. Dad backed the truck into our spot so the bumper reached under the trailer hitch. Despite what I'd said to Dad, walking up to the trailer still made me feel like it was time to relax—the same way I felt when I came home from school.

No apartment I'd ever lived in with Mom had ever been as saturated with the musty smell of disintegrating upholstery, old crumbs, and fast-food grease. The grime lining the window ledges and smashed into the poo-brown carpet was dark enough to predate dinosaurs. The upholstery sported images of bright flowers in teal and orange and avocado green—colors that hadn't been cool since the seventies and were probably questionable then. Besides, the entire trailer was barely the size of the living room in my last apartment with Mom.

When Dad first picked me up, all my instincts told me to at least buy some sterile wipes at the 7-Eleven. But if Dad wanted to live in this hamster box, let him. I didn't want him to get too used to having me around. Mom was always burning incense in our apartment, and I wished I had some now, but I'd left all that stuff at Grandma's when Dad picked me up. I'd barely had room to bring two weeks' worth of clothes. Other luxuries had been out of the question. Mom hadn't left me enough money to keep paying rent, so I'd stashed the rest of our belongings in boxes in Grandma's basement. I left the furniture behind. It was all thrift-store stuff anyway.

Dad slept on the bed at the back, which had cabinets both above and beneath it. We shared the closet, which was about two feet wide and five feet tall. Most of Dad's clothes had gotten stuffed into brown paper bags and chucked into the storage compartments on the outside of the trailer to make room for me. As it was, we were going to have to do laundry in the RV park coin-ops.

I walked along the bench next to the tiny table to climb onto my bed above the hitch. When Dad picked me up, he'd given me that bed like he was doing me a favor. "I have to get into the cabinets by the other bed all the time," he'd said. "I thought you might like to have your own space." But my own space was a three-foot-high slot, barely the size of a twin mattress. At home I'd slept on a queen.

Dad dropped the bag of food onto the table and flipped open a fold-out chair so he wouldn't have to squeeze onto one of the benches beneath my bed. As he rustled out the remaining tacos the smell of hot sauce wafted up to me, making me want to pinch my nose.

"I can't believe you make me live in this thing," I said. "I'm fifteen, and I don't even have a door to close."

"Which means you can't keep boys behind it," Dad said. "It's all part of my brilliant plan."

"But you're a man. It's indecent."

"It's not indecent," Dad said. "You're my daughter."

"For, like, a week."

"No. You've always been my daughter. And you don't need a door. You have a curtain."

I snorted and then swung the curtain closed on him, the metal rings screeching against the bar. Since he could still hear my every breath, it didn't really make a difference.

"Whatever," I said through the curtain. "I should at least have a door to slam when you say crap like that."

"You can go slam the truck door if it makes you feel better."

"Maybe I will."

I thought I might have heard Dad chuckle, but I didn't open the curtain to be sure. I knew I sounded like a brat, but whatever.

I moved over and pulled open the curtains on the front window. Outside, rain coursed down the glass in little streams. I could see trees blowing a few feet away, the leaves obscured by the layers of water.

"I was doing fine at Grandma's, you know," I said. "If I was still there, Mom could find me faster."

"Grandma didn't think she could handle you."

In the three weeks I stayed with Grandma I'd done all her dishes and cooked for her six times. "It's not like I'm so hard to live with," I said.

"I know. I guess I wore her out enough for both of us."

I'd heard Grandma say over the phone to Dad that she didn't want to deal with having "another teenager under her roof," as if I were a particularly nasty breed of dog, the kind she'd had once and sworn never to keep again.

"Were you really that bad?" I pulled the curtains open a couple of inches, peering at him.

He met my eyes. "I don't know. I had a couple of girlfriends she didn't like. And I didn't go to college, which for her was about the end of the world."

"You also married a woman she didn't like."

"Did your Grandma tell you that?"

"Not out loud. But she doesn't like it when Mom takes off and I stay with her."

"Grandma says your mom does that to you a lot."

"It's not like she does it *to* me. I don't mind her going out of town."

"Does she usually tell you where she's going?"

"Yeah," I said. "Sometimes, anyway." I breathed in deep, trying to loosen up. Everything I said made Mom sound bad, when that wasn't how it was. "Grandma doesn't always like you so much either."

Dad laughed. "Is that so?"

I pushed the curtains aside more. "Yeah, sometimes she's mad at Mom, but other times she tells me that it's her responsibility to look after me, since *her son* won't do it." I waved my finger in the air the way Grandma did when she got really worked up.

Dad laughed again. "That sounds like her."

"I guess that responsibility stops after three weeks."

"Go easy on her. She's sixty-eight years old."

"But so what if she doesn't like stuff you did? Why take it out on me?"

"I haven't exactly been a model adult, either. I've disappointed her. She's old and tired. I think she just doesn't want to be a parent anymore."

"That doesn't seem like a choice a parent can make, but I guess some people do anyway." I knew that one would get him, since he'd given the same lecture to Alison this afternoon.

Dad looked down at the table. "Your mom shouldn't have done that to you, but I guess you understand parenting better than she does."

I balled my fists. He'd totally missed the point. "If you think she's such a bad parent, where have *you* been?" I asked.

Dad looked up at me, eyes wide. "Jeez, Ricki. I'm so sorry."

I didn't know how to respond to that. I shouldn't have brought it up. I knew now that Dad wasn't some noble guy off saving the world. But a part of me still hoped there was something else to the story. Maybe he was secretly a criminal, and only Mom knew. Maybe he was just making all this bounty-hunting stuff look normal so I wouldn't know he was working for some secret government agency.

Anything but what I figured the truth must be: that he just hadn't cared about me.

The more we talked about it, the more likely I was to hear that truth. Better to avoid it.

"Grandma wouldn't have had to keep me for long. Mom always comes back." I looked up at the wall at the head of my bed where I'd tacked a picture of Mom and me, and the note I'd found when I came home to our apartment from school for the last time.

Off to california, it said. Take the bus to Grandma's. I'll pick you up soon. I knew that Mom had been talking to a guy, one she met on one of those dumb dating sites. She probably went to visit him. I just hadn't thought she'd be gone so long. Just last month I'd read an article about a woman who'd been dating on-line and disappeared. They found her body in a Dumpster. I tried every day not to think about that.

I should have let the subject drop then, but for some reason I couldn't help picking at it like an itchy scab.

"Must be a real bummer for you to be stuck with me all of a sudden," I said.

Dad smiled at me. "Not at all. I'm happy to have you along. I just wish it was under better circumstances."

"Yeah, well, I guess it can't be helped."

"Seriously. I'm glad you're here. It gives us a chance to really get to know each other."

That was the truth. Dad didn't even have a TV in his trailer—just his audiobooks. No good distractions to turn my brain off.

Dad looked at me like he expected me to say that I was happy to be with him as well, but I hurt too much, so I changed the subject.

"So this Ian guy. What was his last name? Something to do with Shakespeare?"

"Burnham. Like the woods in Macbeth."

"That's the one with the witches, right?"

Dad grinned. "Ah. She is cultured after all."

"'Double, double toil and trouble.' We had to recite that poem for Halloween in the sixth grade."

"Nice to hear they're still teaching the classics."

"Even if I don't know what that wood is?"

"We can work on that. What's your favorite book?" Dad asked.

I squinted up at the ceiling. Didn't have far to look, since it was barely two feet above my face.

"I don't like to read books."

"What?" I could see Dad peering at me over the bunk ledge. That was clearly the wrong answer.

"I don't," I said.

"How can that be? What was the last book you read?"

"I read part of *Ethan Frome*." That wasn't a lie. I read those summaries online.

"That's for school. I mean before that."

"Well, we read *The Catcher in the Rye*. That was for class too, but I guess it was okay."

"What'd you like about it?"

"I liked the way the kid had nowhere to go so he just wandered around making observations about the people he saw." I kind of wanted to be like him, with my lists and my blog. Just not the crazy part.

"See? So you do like to read."

"Well, I didn't hate the book, but it's not as if I read it for fun."

"Sounds like your mom. I couldn't get her to pick up anything thicker than an issue of *Cosmo*."

I rolled over onto my elbows. "Not everything short is shallow. I read the news."

"Like, the newspaper?"

"No. I get my news online."

"So you read about movie stars and things?"

My hands itched toward my pillow—the only immediate throwable object. I scrunched it up instead. "No," I said. "That's soft news. I read the real stuff. About bombings and kidnappings and things. But I'm behind, since Grandma's Internet connection didn't work that well."

Dad looked impressed. "You read about politics?"

"Sure. I can name all the members of the president's cabinet. Can you?"

Dad laughed. "I sure can't. Good for you."

I could name them when I wasn't put on the spot. If Dad actually asked me to, I'd probably forget one.

"Anyway," I said. "This Ian guy. What'd he do?"

Dad cleared his throat. "Jumped bail. Just like the rest of them."

"But why was he arrested in the first place?"

"Doesn't matter. Cal needs him in court, so I'm going to bring him back. Why don't you get your books out of the truck? Don't think I didn't notice that you still have work to do."

Dad gave me one of those looks that meant the conversation was over. It took all my self-control not to stick my tongue out at him. That would be a totally third-grade move, not really good for convincing him I could deal with hearing about skips.

"I mean it," he said. "Go."

I groaned but flipped my legs over the side of the bed and hopped down beside him, nearly whacking my hip on the edge of his folding chair.

If Jamie was here, he'd know what to say to get around Dad. He was really good at talking people into things. He'd find some excuse for us to get out of here. Maybe he could steal his cousin's motorcycle and drive to get me. Then I could ride behind him and breathe him in.

I ran through the rain and hopped up into the cab

with my books. The sun had disappeared behind thick clouds. It'd be setting soon anyway. If I went back into the trailer, Dad would see me working and know that he'd won. But if I stayed here, he'd wonder where I'd gone and then maybe come out here to check up on me. And I'd be sitting here doing my work like a good girl, and he'd feel sorry.

But I didn't start my homework. Instead I spread my notebook across my lap, writing in the dim light.

Ian Burnham is seventeen, I wrote. *And he's already gotten arrested and jumped bail.* I wondered where we'd find him and what he'd be like. Having someone close to my age around had to be an improvement over being alone with Dad—even if he was a skip.

Denver, Colorado.
Days since Mom left: 30.
Distance from Salt Lake City, Utah: 543.16 miles.

4

The first place Dad was going to look for Ian Burnham was his house in Aurora.

"Does Ian live with his parents?" I asked as we drove out, leaving the trailer behind. The morning sun shone off the road, and I blocked the glare with the newspaper Dad had bought me that morning in the trailer-park office. The thing was so big, I had to block the whole window with it if I wanted to read a story at the bottom of the page.

But I had my own story brewing, and I wanted information.

"His aunt has custody," Dad said, "so he was living with her when he got arrested."

"Are his parents dead?"

"His mom's in rehab."

"Like, for alcohol?"

"Like, for drugs."

"So why doesn't he live with his dad, then?"

"The dad's in jail for domestic abuse."

Jeez. That meant Ian had it even worse than me, which at the moment was saying something. "His dad hit his mom?"

"Not that I know of," Dad said. "The parents are divorced. Looks like the dad was living with a girlfriend."

"So, how long has Ian been with his aunt?"

Dad rolled his eyes at me. "I have his legal information, not his biography." Dad patted his clipboard. "I also didn't memorize it."

"Can I see it?"

"No, you can't."

Blah. I'd have to look at it when Dad wasn't around. "Do you really think he's still at his aunt's place?"

"She's the one who paid Cal to post bail, so I'm guessing if he was still there, she'd have dragged him to court herself. But she's out the bail money now, so she might be willing to give me an idea where he's gone. Jilted relatives are my number one source of information. Skips have usually pissed off someone or other. All I have to do is find that person."

I picked up my notebook, but Dad looked meaningfully

down at the uncracked book in my lap—*Ethan Frome* for my past-due report. I'd tried to bury it under the newspaper, but it was peeking out.

I'd have to write that information down later. All this advice would make a great blog post—how to skip bail and not get caught. Don't piss off your relatives. Don't stay home. Don't worry about your mail.

I folded the newspaper, though it didn't seem to crease back together the way it had come. I opened *Ethan Frome* and stared at the title page again. If I made it a goal to get through three pages a day, I might finish the book sometime this century. Today I could do the title page, the dedication, and the first page of the introduction. It was a half page even.

"It's hard to read in here," I said.

"You chose that when you refused to work back at the trailer."

"You could bring the trailer along. Then I could ride in back and work and still not have to be alone all day."

"That's illegal. No one can be in the trailer while it's moving."

"So what? It's not like anyone would know."

"I'd know."

"Are *you* going to turn yourself in?"

"I don't break the law," Dad said. "That's the difference between me and the skips. Now get reading."

"Fine," I said. "I just wanted to talk to you. That's all."

Dad sighed. "Grand theft auto."

"What?"

"Last night you asked me what Burnham did. He's a car thief, up for grand theft auto."

I closed the book again. So much for goals. "And that's why he's dangerous? Because stealing cars sends you to jail for a long time?"

"It's not his first offense, and at seventeen he could get charged as an adult. That means prison time."

"So he probably won't be hanging out at home."

"Right," Dad said. "But it's still the right place to start."

"Do you think he has a gun?"

"No," Dad said. "Most of the people I pick up aren't packing. But I have to treat them all like they are, just in case."

"Why'd you take the job? Cal said you asked for this kind of thing."

Dad was quiet for a long moment. Then he cleared his throat. "Someone's got to find him. Might as well be me."

"That's not the real reason. It's just what you're telling me so I'll drop it."

"See how well that's working?"

"Fine."

Dad looked over at me, still smiling. "You're a hard woman to please. Just like your mom."

I opened my mouth to complain, but Dad waved a hand at me. "Don't start. That wasn't an insult. There's nothing wrong with arguing, even if it does make my life more difficult. At least it means you're thinking."

I didn't know how to respond to that.

"Do you think we'll get in a car chase?"

"You think that would be fun?"

"I don't know. I was wondering if you get in a lot of chases."

"Foot chases, yes. Car chases, no."

"But what if your skip jumps in a car and drives away?"

"Then I keep tailing him. I'll even follow him at slow speeds. But high-speed chases hurt bystanders more often than not. Even if they don't, a lot of times the damages cost more than the bounty was worth."

"So, do a lot of skips get away?"

Dad wobbled his head from side to side. "Eh," he said. "I probably bring in eight out of ten. Some of them get picked up by law enforcement before I get the chance. Some run out of the country, and I can't follow them then."

"Why not?"

"Because it's against the law."

Right. I looked out the window, watching the road

rush away beneath us. Tangled weeds on the shoulder slid by in a blur.

"So you're really good at finding people, then."

"Not bad. That's why Cal gives me so much work."

I turned and looked at him. "So are you looking for Mom?"

"No," he said. He didn't even take a moment to think about it.

"Why not?" I asked. "If you found Mom, then you wouldn't have to deal with me anymore. You could have the whole trailer all to yourself."

"I don't mind dealing with you. Like I said last night, it's nice to have a chance to get to know you."

I scrunched down in my seat and rested my feet on the dash. "That's not the point," I said. "She's never been gone this long before. What if something happened to her?"

I was pretty sure Mom was fine—she always scraped through. And the fact that kidnappings and murders made the news also meant they were rare. But the nagging thoughts in the back of my mind were really starting to bug me. I just wanted to find her so I could stop wondering.

"Look," Dad said, "you know how I have to sign paperwork with a bail bondsman before I go looking for a skip?"

"So?"

Dad gave me a warning look. "That's because people who take bail bonds sign away their constitutional rights to the bondsman. They give him the right to track them down and arrest them if they don't show up in court, and then he signs that right over to me so I can find them for him."

"So what?"

"So your mom hasn't signed away her rights to me, or anyone I work for. I'm not authorized to go looking for her, which means I have no right to bring her back."

"I don't see why you can't look for Mom on the side."

"You know how strong willed your mother is. You're just like her. Trying to drag her back here before she's ready would only cause more trouble for all of us. She's got a right not to be found."

"What about my right to have a mother?" I asked. As soon as I said it I was sorry. I hadn't meant to turn the conversation back to me.

But Dad didn't respond. He just stared at the road slipping away beneath us, tightening his grip on the steering wheel.

We'd been in the truck for less than twenty minutes when Dad pulled up to a house in a residential neighborhood. He climbed out of the cab, walked up to the house, and pounded his fist on the door.

I sat close to the window, watching. When Dad went to get Alison, he'd knocked on the door and asked for her. But he said he sometimes had to break in and drag people out. Dad said that was legal for licensed bounty hunters, but it still sounded dangerous to me. I half wanted to see it happen, but only if everything turned out okay in the end.

Dad waited a second and then banged on the door again. When no one answered, he walked to the side of the house and peered over into the backyard like a cop in a movie.

There it was. A glimpse of the superhero dad my eight-year-old self wanted. My dad could break into other people's houses. My dad had handcuffs and chains—and not for weird, kinky reasons either. My dad had the power to drag people to jail.

I wondered if Batman's daughter would have felt left out too.

As Dad came back around the house, he glanced in the window and then waved to someone inside. A moment later the front door swung open, and a woman in a V-neck shirt and tapered jeans stepped out. She was probably the same age as Mom, and she dressed like she was still in high school, just like Mom did. It always made me mad when Mom shopped in the juniors section, even if it did mean I could borrow her clothes.

I opened the door of the truck so I could hear what Dad was saying.

". . . Ian Burnham," he said, his deep voice carrying. "You seen him?"

"He ran off a couple of weeks ago," the woman said. "Haven't seen him since."

"You know where he might have gone?"

I hopped out of the cab. This wasn't turning into a drag-'em-out scenario, so I was safe.

The woman shook her head again. Dad stepped closer, standing up a little taller. "Are you his guardian?"

"I was. You with the police?"

"No, ma'am. I'm a bail enforcement agent. I'm here because Mr. Burnham didn't show up for his court date. If you're his guardian, you must be pretty upset at losing that bail money."

She crossed her arms in front of her. "Nothing I can do about it now. He stole my car and fifty dollars from my wallet when he left. I shouldn't have put up the collateral for the bondsman, but I felt so sorry for Ian because of his mom. Now my damn house is on the line."

"That's a tough spot to be in. That's what I'm here about, though. I'd like to see you keep your collateral. I just need you to help me find Ian."

As I walked up behind Dad, the woman looked over

Dad's shoulder at me. Then she reached into her pocket and pulled out a lighter and a cigarette.

"I don't know how much help I can be," she said.

"You get your car back yet?"

"Asshole abandoned it downtown. Got it back last week."

Dad didn't look too happy about that, probably because tracking the stolen car would have given him something to go on.

Ian's aunt lit up her cigarette, took a long drag, and blew smoke up at the eaves.

I wondered if stealing his aunt's car counted as grand theft auto. I mean, Jamie borrowed his cousin's motorcycle all the time, which I guess was technically stealing, since he didn't ask first. But he always gave it back.

"You must have some idea where he would have gone. Any information is a help."

She waved a dismissive hand at Dad. "You could check his cousin's place. I called up there, but they might be lying to me."

"Got an address?"

The woman nodded and disappeared into the entryway.

Dad glared over his shoulder at me, acknowledging me for the first time. "I told you to stay in the truck."

"No you didn't."

"Maybe not specifically. It should go without saying."
Dad gave me a look like he wasn't sure what to do
with me, but then the woman reappeared with a piece
of paper.

"Here's the address," she said. "If you find him, don't
bring him back here."

"You got it," Dad said, offering her a card. "I'll be
taking him right to the warden. If you see or hear from
him, though, give me a call. Don't tell him I'm coming.
Just let me know where he is."

She took the card.

"Thanks for your help," Dad said. He took me by the
arm, and we walked back toward the truck.

I climbed into the cab, speaking quietly so the woman
wouldn't hear. "She wasn't very helpful."

Dad shrugged. "She gave us a lead. And she's pissed
enough that she's probably not covering for him. If she
hears from him, she'll call."

"So where are we going next?"

"Laramie, Wyoming," Dad said. He looked at the
address, grabbed his GPS and clicked some buttons.
"Two-and-a-half-hour drive. We should pick up the trailer,
in case we get another lead farther off."

"What is with cousins? Isn't that where Alison was
staying too?"

Dad nodded. "Happens a lot. A cousin is a distant

enough relative that it seems no one will look for you there, but still close enough that he lets you stay."

"I guess," I said. Mom and Dad were both only children, so I didn't have any cousins. Anna had thirty-five of them. I'd been to a couple of her family get-togethers, but they always felt more like block parties to me.

I pulled out my notebook and added to my list of things not to do on the run. *Don't stay with your cousin. That's not far enough away.* Then I opened to the page where I'd written Ian's name. *Ian's dad's in jail, and his mom's in rehab. Life sucks for him.* That last bit wasn't strictly an observation, but it was a small enough leap that I let myself slide. Of course, if I wanted to blog about Ian, I'd need to change his name. Maybe I'd call him "the woods." Dad would get a kick out of that.

Dad pulled out his clipboard to make some notes of his own. "Get going on your homework," he said. "You haven't even started for today."

I held up *Ethan Frome.* "This book is seriously unreadable."

"Then work on something else. Read me your math assignment, and I'll try to help you through it."

"It's algebra," I said. "Doesn't make a very good read-aloud."

"I took algebra once, if you can believe it."

"I don't remember the math I took last year. How do you remember algebra from high school?"

"I'm a smart guy. We'll figure it out together."

As I read the chapter intro for conic sections, Dad drove us back to the RV park to hitch up. Then we headed up I-25 to I-80 West—the direction of Salt Lake.

"You could drive me back to Grandma's on your way."

Dad laughed. "That's only, what? A twelve-hour detour?"

"Six."

"I mean round trip."

"I'm sure Ian will wait."

Dad rolled his eyes at me, and even I couldn't help but laugh.

The phone rang, then, beeping steadily from the dash. Dad punched a button, turning it on speaker.

"This is Max," he said.

"Hey," a girl's voice said. "Is Ricki there?"

Dad's eyes widened, and he turned toward me. I grabbed the phone and turned the speaker off.

"Hello?" I said, putting the phone to my ear.

"Ricki?"

"Anna?"

"Ricki! Oh my gosh, how are you?"

Hearing Anna's voice felt almost as good as hearing Jamie's. "All right, I guess. Aren't you at school?"

"Yeah. I'm calling from the bathroom. I just checked my e-mail in computer class. Is this your dad's cell?"

"Yeah," I said, "I'm in the truck with him now." I made a point not to look at Dad. He was probably ticked that I'd given out the number, so this call from Anna might be my last. I wished I didn't have to talk with him listening in.

"Have you heard from your mom?"

"Not yet."

"What a bitch. I can't believe it."

I leaned my head back against the seat. Hearing Anna call Mom a bitch actually made me feel better. It wasn't like when Dad said bad things about her. It's the best friend's job to be pissed when her friend gets screwed over.

"How's Jamie doing?" I asked. "He hasn't forgotten about me, has he?"

Anna was quiet for a second. "I haven't really seen him much."

I was tempted to ask her to go with him to homecoming, since I knew he wasn't interested in her. She'd also let me cut back in on him when I returned, no hard feelings or anything. Anna was like that. But Mom always said not to trust any girl with your boyfriend, especially a best friend.

"If you see him, tell him to e-mail me."

"He hasn't?"

"No." Damn, it hurt to admit that.

"Bastard. You're too good for him, you know."

"Just find out if he's seeing someone else, okay?"

"If he is, I'm so telling her about his gonorrhea."

"The one you just made up?"

"That's the one."

"Are things okay with your dad? Do I need to give him imaginary illnesses too? I bet I could come up with a good one."

I smiled. Anna always had my back. But there was only so much I could say with Dad sitting right there. "Things are okay. I can't wait to get back, though."

"I can't wait for you to come home. Do you have any idea what it's like to sit through bio without you? I'm stuck next to Amy Allbridge now. Every day I spend an hour watching her tattoo herself with a paper clip and a ballpoint pen."

"Ew. Hasn't Ms. Langley noticed?"

"Yeah. Amy's on her third paper clip. I don't know why Ms. Langley thinks taking the paper clips away is going to make her stop."

I closed my eyes. I should be there with Anna. We should be watching this together.

"Anyway, I've got to get back to class. Text me soon, 'kay?"

"I will if I can," I said. "Dad's kind of picky about his phone."

"All right. Love you. Bye!"

And then she was gone. I stuck the phone back on the dash, still not looking at Dad. We drove in silence for a few miles, until I couldn't take it anymore.

"Are you mad at me for giving out your number?" I asked.

Dad sighed. "It's a work phone. You should have asked me. I can't have your friends calling on it all the time."

"I only talked for, like, two minutes."

"I know. Just don't give it out to anyone else, all right?"

"Okay." That was easy to promise, since I'd already given it to everyone.

"And if anyone else calls, you can talk for a few minutes, but that's it."

"Can I make one more call?"

"Not right now."

Jamie hadn't called yet even though he had the number. Calling him would probably look desperate, anyway.

"Read that math assignment to me. We're going to figure this out."

I pulled out the book, mentally thinking of the kinds of illnesses Anna might assign to Dad. I'd suggest laryngitis.

Laramie, Wyoming.
Days since Mom left: 30.
Distance from Salt Lake City, Utah: 399.2 miles.

5

It turned out working on graphing problems was really hard when one of us couldn't see the graphs. After trying to describe the lines to Dad, I started sketching them in the condensation at the edges of the windshield. They weren't very exact but got the point across.

We pulled into Laramie around eleven o'clock. Everything about the town was brown—the shrubs, the hills, the buildings, even the shop signs—like someone had built it to match a sepia photograph.

"Want a milkshake?" Dad asked.

My stomach growled, even though I was really tired of fast food.

"Maybe a sandwich, too. I could drop you at a burger place and then pick you up on our way out."

"You can't just leave me at some restaurant."

"Why not? You can work on that math."

"Because I'm your daughter, not your dog."

"I wouldn't leave a dog alone in a restaurant."

"You know what I mean."

"Fine," Dad said. "We'll stop for food on our way out. But this time you stay in the truck. I mean it."

The cousin's house was in a rattier neighborhood, full of overgrown lawns and broken-down cars. Dad pulled on his bounty-hunting persona as he walked up to the door, taking long, deliberate steps.

As he pounded on the door, a guy in jeans hoisted himself over the backyard fence.

I gasped. The guy looked a little older than me, with black hair and olive skin. His hips pivoted like a gymnast's as he twisted his legs over the fence and dropped feet first into a neighbor's yard.

That had to be Ian Burnham.

I kicked open my door and yelled at Dad. "He went that way!" I pointed to the house next door, and Dad jerked into action. He sprinted around the corner to the fence, moving faster than I would have thought a dad could. He jerked at the neighbor's gate, but it didn't open immediately, so Dad grabbed onto the top of the fence and pulled himself up, throwing one leg over.

The fence scraped down his leg as Dad tossed

himself into the neighbor's yard—much less gracefully than Ian had. I watched the fence tops for movement but saw nothing.

Out of sight in the neighbor's yard, anything could happen. If Dad got hurt, how would I even know? What should I do if he didn't come back? Call 911?

I held my breath. This was almost like watching an episode of *Cops*, except that if someone got killed, no one could turn off the camera.

When Dad didn't come back, I started to wonder if I should go after him. Maybe Ian had knifed him. Or maybe it was nothing—maybe the neighbor had caught Dad in his yard and Dad had to stop to explain. Then again, the neighbor might have pointed a gun at him. There were people like that—people who'd shoot an intruder before asking questions.

My hands itched for the cell phone Dad had left Velcroed to the dash. I could call the cops. Make them go look.

Right then the fence swung open and Dad appeared, dragging the skip with him. Dad didn't look shot or knifed. I let out the breath I'd been holding.

Dad held Ian's arms behind his back as he brought him out of the yard. On the news, people usually kept their heads down when they were being arrested, trying to hide their faces. Not Ian. He kept his head thrown back, his chin thrust forward like he was going to use it to catch a fall. His eyes glanced around, like he was looking for a direction to make his escape. This skip was nothing like Alison. He wasn't going to come easy.

Ian wore a long-sleeved shirt that fit tightly through the chest and across his arms, showing off his pecs and biceps. The shirt had a straight-edger symbol on it, like one that Jamie's friend Jake used to wear before he got beat up for it.

As they approached the car, both Ian and Dad looked at me. I hadn't closed the door, so nothing but air stood between us. Ian met my eyes and nodded. I wasn't sure what to do. Was it safe to nod back?

Dad raised his eyebrows at me and looked pointedly at my open door. I reached out and closed it as Dad pushed Ian against the side of the truck, holding his cuffs in place with one hand and frisking him with the other.

Ian's face pressed against the back passenger window. He had dark eyelashes—long like a girl's—and a scar across his cheek, maybe from a piece of glass or a knife fight. His dark eyes twitched, watching me through the glass as Dad tossed a Zippo lighter, some cigarettes, and a wallet onto the sidewalk. The cigarettes weren't very straight-edge. Maybe he just thought the shirt looked cool.

I probably should have looked away, but I couldn't

make myself. Ian held eye contact with me, but with his face being all squishy, I couldn't read his expression. Was he sizing me up? Did he think I was a fugitive too?

Dad pulled Ian aside and opened the back passenger door. Ian threw his weight backward, leveraging his feet on the bottom of the door to keep Dad from forcing him inside. Dad had him cornered, though, and put pressure on the back of Ian's knees so they buckled and he fell onto the bench.

In no time, Dad had Ian's feet and cuffs chained to the floor bolt. The whole time, Ian kept his head back, his face only a foot from mine. I curled my toes in my shoes. This was exactly the kind of person I'd always thought Dad picked up. Someone tough, someone who didn't back down. I couldn't take my eyes off him.

Dad slammed the side door. He picked up Ian's belongings from the sidewalk and locked them in one of the utility boxes in the side of the truck, then walked around to the driver's-side door.

Ian half smiled at me from the back seat.

"Hi," I said.

Ian leaned forward, resting his elbows on his knees and his chin on his cuffed hands. The chain attached to his cuffs stretched between his knees to the floor bolt. Dad hadn't left him much slack. "Hey," he said.

He didn't ask me who I was, but I still felt the need to

explain. "I'm Ricki," I said. "I'm . . . his daughter." I wasn't sure what to call Dad. The bounty hunter? Mr. Maxwell? Was he on a first-name basis with skips?

Dad pulled open the driver's-side door. "Turn around," he barked at me. "Get back to your homework." Then he focused on Ian. "You. Leave her alone."

"Yes, sir," Ian said, turning his half smile at Dad. "Whatever you say."

Dad climbed into the driver's seat and adjusted the rearview mirror so he could watch Ian while he drove. Then he picked up my math book and handed it to me.

"Get to work," he said. "I mean it."

"I thought you were going to help me."

"Do as much as you can now, and I'll help you tonight."

I rolled my eyes. I guess Dad felt like he had to be terse around skips, since he didn't have a badge or anything to make them respect him. I wanted to argue, but I didn't want Ian to think I was some kind of baby, fighting with my dad about homework. So instead I opened up my math book as if it'd been my idea to do the work in the first place.

We stopped at a fast-food place on our way back to the freeway. The trailer wouldn't fit through most drive-thrus, so Dad parked in the lot and then waved an arm at me. "I'm going to use the toilet. You come in and grab some food."

"Nah," I said. "I'm not hungry." Okay, so I was starving. But I couldn't talk to Ian unless I got him alone.

"I'm hungry," Ian said.

"I didn't ask you. Come on, Ricki."

"Give me a break, bounty man," Ian said. "You can't starve me to death. I'll sue."

"It's a two-and-a-half-hour drive. You'll live." Dad gave me a look. "I'm going in," he said. "You can starve if you want, but I want you out of the car."

"But I've got homework to do," I said, opening *Ethan Frome*. "I'm really starting to get into this book."

I heard Ian chuckle from the back seat. Dad wasn't buying it either. He just stood there, watching me like there was no way in hell he was going to let me stay.

So I climbed out of the car and shut the door on Ian, so he wouldn't be able to hear. Persuading Dad was way easier when skips weren't listening. "You're not going to leave him in there, are you?" I asked. "What if something happens?"

Dad raised his eyebrows. "Like what, exactly?"

"Well," I said, "what if he manages to reach the gear shift from the back seat and rolls the truck into the street? Or what if someone comes by and he convinces them that some psycho's taken him prisoner and they let him go?"

Dad looked over my shoulder at Ian. "Seems unlikely," he said. "I have to leave skips alone sometimes when I'm tracking by myself."

"But you're not by yourself now. You have me. And I can watch him."

I expected Dad to refuse out of hand, but instead he watched me silently for a minute.

"What?" I asked.

"I told you I didn't want you getting involved with my work."

"And I told *you* that if you didn't want me involved, you shouldn't drag me along. If you don't think I'm capable of watching a guy who's *chained* in a *truck*—who's so secure you're not worried about leaving him *alone*—then you might as well drop me off with Child and Family Services."

I held my breath. That last bit was taking it a little far. He might decide I was right about the Child Services part.

But he didn't.

"Okay, fine," Dad said. "I'll bring you back some food. But you watch him from *outside* the truck, okay?"

"Okay," I said. "I promise."

Dad gave me a sharp nod and then headed into the restaurant, looking back at me once over his shoulder.

When he was gone, I stood outside the truck, wondering what to do. I mean, I looked like an idiot standing there in the middle of a parking space. I could at least open the door and talk to Ian. Dad hadn't forbidden that. If you weren't supposed to leave dogs alone in locked vehicles, you probably shouldn't do it with skips, either.

I stepped over to the driver's-side door—opposite Ian's seat—and cracked it open.

"If you're really not hungry, could you get me a burger?" Ian asked.

"Um," I said, "I'm supposed to watch you. Sorry."

"Eh. It's cool."

I leaned against the edge of the open door so my head was half inside the truck. "I like your shirt," I said.

"Really?"

"I like metal too."

Ian smiled, like he was actually impressed. "I wouldn't have pegged you for a straight-edger."

"I'm not," I said. "But a friend of mine is."

The straight-edger scene is kind of different in Salt Lake. In most places it's just a group of teenagers who listen to metal music and don't drink or do drugs or smoke, which is cool. But in Utah it's turned into kind of a gang. The straight-edgers there are always beating people up and graffitiing stuff, which Jake thought was stupid. So he wore the shirt to try to show people you didn't have to

63

be all violent to be a straight-edger—until some guy decided to take it out on him by bashing his head into a sound wall.

"That's cool," Ian said.

I smiled. Ian, who took an arrest in stride with his head up and his eyes open, thought *I* was cool. "So are you doing okay back there? It doesn't look very comfortable to be chained up like that."

"Yeah, these chains kind of chafe. You think you could unlock me?"

"No," I said.

Ian grinned. "Kidding. So what are you doing here, anyway? Your old man bring you along a lot?"

"No," I said. "Just this last week. My mom sort of took off, so I didn't have anywhere else to go." I don't know why I told him that. Maybe I thought he would understand, since his parents were so messed up. I expected Ian to say something about how sorry he was, or about how awful it was to be left.

"Lucky you," he said.

"What's that supposed to mean?"

"It means good riddance. Parents are a pain in the ass."

"Yeah, but now I'm stuck here, when all my friends are back in Utah."

"So why don't you go back?"

"I don't have anywhere to stay.

"Whatever. Get an apartment."

"With what money?"

"Get a job."

"You make this sound easy."

"Look," Ian said. Stretching his chains tight so his hands just barely reached the back of the seat, he leaned toward me, looking at me intensely. "Sometimes you've got to grab the bull by the balls."

"Won't that get me kicked in the face?"

Ian laughed. "Sometimes. It got me chained in a truck. But at least I'm trying."

I wasn't sure what I thought about that. I liked the idea of hitching a ride back home and living my life again, with or without Mom. But there were so many details to worry about. I'd have to have some place to stay, at least while I was looking for a job. Maybe I could get Anna to work on her parents for me.

"So was it bull balls that got you charged with grand theft auto?"

Ian laughed. "You know my whole history or what?"

I shrugged. "My dad has a file on you."

"What's it say?"

"That your mom's in rehab and your dad's in jail."

"That it?"

"And that your aunt had custody of you. We drove by there this morning."

"And she helped you find me."

"A little."

"That figures."

He looked down at his shoes, and I watched the sunlight sliding in the window and glancing off his profile.

"I'm sorry about your family," I said.

"Look, girl. What was your name?"

"Ricki," I said. "It's short for Erica."

"Look, Ricki, you don't need to be sorry. Your mom leaving, my mom being a druggie, that's just life. In life sometimes other people are going to give you shit. But when they do, you just make shitballs and toss them right back. Understand?"

"Yeah," I said. "Thanks." I leaned against the edge of the truck, trying to make sense of it. But here was Ian, chained in the very truck I'd been whining and miserable about, and not even blinking an eye. So maybe he had something there.

Then Dad walked toward us, carrying a brown paper bag under his arm, grease stains soaking through the bottom. He gave me a look as he approached. I stepped away from the door, and he opened it the rest of the way, sticking the food on the front seat.

As I moved to walk around to the front, Dad grabbed my arm and tugged me around the back of the trailer, out of Ian's earshot.

"What?" I asked.

"What the hell were you doing?"

I wanted to tell him I was grabbing the bull by the balls, but he wouldn't get it. Instead I squinted at him. "I was watching Ian, just like you said I could."

"I told you to stay out of the truck."

"I did. I just opened the door a little."

Dad crossed his arms across his chest. "How many times do I have to tell you not to talk to skips?"

My mouth fell open. "I was just watching him. It's not like I unchained him."

"But I asked you not to talk to skips, and you deliberately disobeyed me."

"I have to *obey* you? I thought we went over how I'm not your dog."

"Ricki, I ask you to do these things for your safety. Skips aren't ordinary people. They're criminals."

"But Ian's just a guy. He's only a little bit older than me." He was also probably the toughest guy I'd ever met, but I didn't figure Dad would appreciate that either.

"Oh, no," Dad said. "You can't think of him that way. This isn't some kid you met at school. He's in very serious trouble, and you will be too, if you aren't careful."

"I did exactly what you told me to do—watched him and stayed out of the truck. If you want me to be silent so you can pretend I'm not here, fine. But don't expect me to ignore your skips just because you do." That wasn't exactly shitballing, but it was a start.

I spun around and ran back to my seat in the cab, where I knew Dad wouldn't chew me out anymore. For once his stiffness in front of the skips could work in my favor.

Dad climbed into the driver's side and shoved the paper bag at me, leaving a grease smear across the bench seat. I dug some fries out of the top.

"So, bounty man," Ian said behind me. "What'd you bring me?"

"Nothing," Dad said. "But I'm sure the prison food will be delicious."

I didn't see why he had to be mean. I turned around, extending a fry to Ian. "Want some?"

Ian smiled, shrugging his cuffed arms. "Guess you'll have to feed me," he said, licking his lips.

My eyes widened, killing my chances of playing it cool. Ian could have fed himself if he bent over a little. That wasn't the point.

"He can eat when we get back to Denver," Dad said sharply. "You turn around."

I popped the fry into my own mouth, smiling at Ian.

He grinned back, and I turned around slowly in my seat, delaying obedience.

As we pulled onto the freeway, Dad focused on the merging traffic. I heard Ian exhale, and hot air puffed over my shoulders, blowing down the back of my shirt. I tried not to react visibly, setting my fries on the seat and looking intently at my algebra. The pages had graphs on them covered in parabolas, but every time I tried to make my own graph it came out looking like a line. I was sure I'd missed something, but Ian sitting behind me made it hard to concentrate on figuring out what.

"So," Ian said, "is it 'Take Your Daughter to Work' day?"

"Sure," Dad said.

I leaned back in my seat a little farther, bench springs creaking. I could hear Ian breathing behind me, his smell drifting across the seat between us. Ms. Langley, my bio teacher back home, said that attraction was a chemical thing based on facial features, anatomy, and smell. It had been that way with Jamie—I'd started liking him when he gave me a ride home on his cousin's motorcycle, and I was all pressed behind him, breathing him in.

"Lean back, buddy," Dad said, and I heard the bench seat creak. "Don't think about trying anything. You don't mess with an armed man's daughter."

I wondered then if Dad actually carried a gun on his person. I knew he had them locked in the truck, but that wouldn't help much in a confrontation with a dangerous skip.

"If you're going to be like that," I said, "why don't you go back to leaving me with the trailer?"

"Girl's got a point," Ian said.

Dad's eyebrows sprang together so fast that I thought they might conjoin. "Shut up," Dad said. "Unless you want me to gag you."

"Are you allowed to do that?" I asked.

Dad gave me another hard look. "You do your homework."

I turned back to my book, drawing yet another axis on my graph paper. "I don't see why I'll ever need conic sections, anyway."

"You probably won't," Dad said. "It's the diploma that counts."

"I don't have a diploma," Ian said.

"You're making my point."

I shrugged. "I still don't get why they make us do this."

Dad nodded. "Get back to old Ethan, then."

"Ethan Frome," I said, "is a weak-willed pansy who couldn't make a decision to save his life."

"How do you know that if you haven't read the book yet?"

"I read the CliffsNotes."

Dad gave me another look. "Where'd you get those?"

"Online."

"You've ruined the book for yourself. No wonder you're bored."

"What's to ruin? Ethan doesn't like his wife at all, so I don't get why he stays with her. If he hadn't, they'd all have been better off for it."

Dad leaned back in his seat, flexing his hands on the wheel. "But he had an obligation to her. So he had to stay."

As if Dad knew anything about marital obligations. "Whatever."

"I think that other chick should have ditched him, anyway," Ian said from the back. "She was too good for him."

Dad and I were both silent for a moment. I looked over my shoulder at him. "Mattie, you mean?"

"Right, that chick. She totally didn't need to stick around with that punk. If she'd gone, she wouldn't have ended up all crippled in the end."

I turned around to face him. "She gets *crippled*?"

"Sure," Ian said. "I thought you said you read the CliffsNotes."

"I didn't get all the way through."

Dad shook his head. "My own daughter can't even finish a set of CliffsNotes."

"It was a library computer. I had a time limit."

"Still."

I turned sideways, lifting my knee onto the seat and leaning against the truck door to get a better look at Ian. "I can't believe you've read *Ethan Frome*."

Ian smirked. "I went to school once too."

"Didn't graduate, though," Dad said.

"How would you know, old man? Is that in your file?"

Dad chuckled. "You told us so a minute ago."

"Oh. Whatever. I might have graduated if they gave us decent books to read."

"And what, in your opinion, is a decent book?" Dad asked.

"Hell, I don't know. *The Shining* was a pretty freaky movie. Must have been a good book."

Dad sniffed. I could tell he wasn't impressed.

"Regardless," Dad said. "Algebra or *Ethan Frome*. Get on it. Now."

"Jeez," Ian said. "Someone needs to get laid."

Dad slammed on the brakes and jerked the truck off the road. I bounced sideways in my seat, whacking my head on the window.

The truck lurched along the shoulder for a few feet and then stopped. I expected Dad to turn around and slug Ian, but instead he pulled on my shoulder, tilting me back in my seat, his eyes stretched wide with horror.

My hand went to my forehead. I thought I might be bleeding, but when I turned to see my reflection in the side mirror, I saw a pink spot on my temple, nothing more.

"I'm so sorry," Dad said. "Are you okay?"

"Yeah," I said. "I'm fine."

I pulled at my seat belt. It should have locked up or something, but I guessed the truck was too old.

Dad and Ian were both staring at me.

"Look, can we just go?" I asked. "I don't get why you stopped in the first place."

"Just don't fall asleep or nothing," Ian said. "If you've got a concussion, you might not wake up."

"You," Dad said, turning around to face Ian. "Shut your mouth. Disrespect me again, and you're gagged. Clear?"

"You sound just like *my* old man."

"There's a common element in those two relationships," Dad said. "And it sure isn't me." He gave my forehead one last look. I could feel a bruise forming, but it didn't feel concussion-bad.

I dug out my novel. As Dad pulled back onto the road I muttered, "I'm the common element with both of my parents. Maybe that's why they both walked out on me."

Dad sighed, but he wasn't going to get into it with me now. Not in front of Ian. If I thought he would, I'd never have said that out loud.

I wasn't more than a page in when I felt Ian's knees pressing into my back through the seat. I could feel his body heat through the disintegrated padding.

I turned to face my window, catching Ian's eye in the side mirror. He looked up at my forehead like he was checking to see if I was okay. And then at the same moment, we both smiled.

Another breath drifted over my neck, directed and cool, as if Ian was blowing on it deliberately. The only kind of contact we could have locked up in here with my dad.

Cheyenne, Wyoming.
Days since Mom left: 30.
Distance from Salt Lake City, Utah: 441.44 miles.

6

Dad stopped for gas in Cheyenne, between Laramie and Denver, right where we had to switch freeways.

"Come on, Ricki," he said. "Get yourself inside."

I looked at the gas station. Dad didn't like the way I'd watched Ian last time so, unfair or not, there was no way he was going to let me help now. But I still wanted to talk to Ian—to know more about him.

I climbed out of the car.

"We just ate," I said. "I don't need anything."

"Well, I'm going to use the bathroom, so you get something for later, and don't go back to the truck until I'm done."

The bathroom door was on the outside of the building,

so Dad waited for me to go into the store before he went inside.

The cashier must have seen my hesitation, because she leaned over the counter toward me. "Can I help you, honey?"

Her pink hair was piled on top of her head, and she had on these little round glasses that gave her owl eyes.

I was still pissed at Dad. That's the only way I know to explain what I did next.

"No, thanks," I said. Then I walked back out to the truck and climbed into the cab.

Ian shook his head at me. "You supposed to be here? Isn't your dad going to freak?"

I shrugged. "Probably. Got any shitballs handy?"

Ian laughed. I'd impressed him.

I squinted at him over my shoulder. "Can I ask you a question?"

He shrugged an arm-twisted shrug. "Why not?"

"Did you do it?"

"Do what?"

"Grand theft auto."

Ian leaned forward. "That's a very personal question," he said. He dropped his chin, looking me in the eyes.

I nodded. "Well?"

He jerked his chin in the direction of my journal. "So I'll show you mine if you show me yours."

76

"Show you what?"

"You're taking notes for your dad, right? I saw you writing down stuff about me. What are you, the secretary?"

I looked down at a split in the seat where the foam poked through, then picked at the edge of it with my finger. "He keeps his own notes. I just like to list things."

"Huh," Ian said. "Well, that's cool."

"You really think so?"

"Yeah," Ian said. "If I wrote things down, I wouldn't forget so much."

"Like your court dates?"

"Nah. I missed those on purpose."

I looked toward the bathroom, but the door was still closed. No sign of Dad yet.

"You didn't answer my question," I said.

"You want to know if I stole those cars?"

I blinked at him. So there'd been more than one car. Did that make him guilty? "Yeah," I said.

"I'm not sure I should tell you. I mean, you're the bounty man's daughter, right? They might call you as a witness or something."

"No one will have to know that I know."

"I pled innocent."

"But then you didn't show up for your hearing."

"Hell no I didn't show up. I'm a poor guy with a record. You think they were going to let me off?"

"That depends. Did you do it?"

Ian laughed from deep in his chest, and the skin on my arms tingled. I wondered what I could say to make him laugh like that again.

"You think that makes a difference?" he asked. "What kind of shelter has the bounty man got around you, anyway?"

I shrugged. "Fine, don't tell me." I'd learned from Anna that the fastest way to get someone to tell you something is to back off and tell them they don't have to share. Tell them it's up to them, and they'll spill their guts all over your shoes.

"Would you still talk to me if I did it?" he asked, his face growing serious.

I thought about that for a second. "Yes," I said.

"But only as long as I'm cuffed in the back seat."

"No," I said. For some reason I wanted him to trust me. Maybe because Dad didn't. "If you did it, you probably had a good reason."

Ian laughed again, more bitterly this time. "Sorry, sweetheart. It's not that I don't believe you, but I wouldn't want to make you an accessory."

I turned my back to him, reaching for my door handle. "Whatever," I said.

"Hey, don't be like that," he said. "Do you think I did it?"

I turned back to him and held his gaze. Did I think he did it? He didn't seem like a bad person, but he did seem like the kind of person who acted first and ran away from consequences later.

"Yes," I said. "You won't tell me if you did it, and I think that means you did."

Ian nodded, neither of us blinking. My heart pounded faster, and I held my breath as shivers ran over me. "Does that matter?" he asked.

I jumped as Dad jerked open the driver's-side door. I hadn't even seen him approach. Ian settled back in his seat, and I whipped around in mine. I expected Dad to chew me out for not waiting for him in the store, but he just glared, first at me, then at Ian. He climbed into the cab and pulled his sunflower seeds out of the glove box, grabbed a gas card off his clipboard, and walked around to the pump.

Ian leaned forward in his seat.

"Hey, bounty man," he said. "I gotta pee."

Dad nodded at him but took his time running his card through the pump and putting the nozzle in the gas tank.

A girl in a University of Wyoming sweatshirt pulled up at the next row of pumps, giving us a dirty look. Looking back, I could see that the trailer blocked all three pumps in our row.

"Shouldn't you pull back?" I yelled at Dad.

Dad shrugged. "Then we'd block the driveway. We'll only be another minute."

The girl left her car running and headed into the station.

"Hey, bounty man," Ian said again. "You don't want me to go on your seat, do you?"

The thought of smelling Ian's urine all the way to Denver made me want to heave. I glared at him, but he grinned back. "Kidding," he said, in a voice quiet enough that only I could hear.

Dad walked around to the passenger side of the truck and opened the back door, unchaining Ian's feet. He pulled another length of chain out from under the seat and hooked it to Ian's cuffs, pulling it taut. "Come on out, then," he said.

As Ian climbed out of the truck, Dad stepped back, letting go of a length of chain so Ian could walk in front of him. Ian looked like a dog on a leash.

Dad and Ian walked toward the building. Dad opened the bathroom door and checked inside. I climbed out of the truck to watch them, leaning against the side of the gas pump.

Dad took the cuffs off Ian's wrists but hooked another on his ankle, so he'd still be attached to the chain. As Ian walked into the bathroom, he bumped against Dad, putting a hand on his shoulder to steady himself. Dad's hand went to his side, but Ian just smiled at him and slipped into the bathroom. I wondered if Dad really had a gun in his pocket.

Dad forced the chain under the door and closed Ian in, keeping hold of the leash. A Jeep pulled up to the parking spaces by the station door, and the driver gave Dad a strange look as he walked into the store. Dad gave the guy a nod but didn't explain himself.

While we waited for Ian, I grabbed a squeegee and wiped the bug splatter off the windshield. The truck was so tall I had to climb up onto the fender to reach the windshield. It wasn't that I wanted to help. I was just sick of looking at grasshopper guts.

As I finished I heard Dad knocking on the bathroom door. "Come on," he yelled. "Let's get moving."

A moment later the door swung open, and Ian came out of the bathroom with his hands up, chain dragging on the concrete floor behind him.

"Hands together," Dad said, reaching toward Ian with the cuffs.

Ian turned toward Dad and stuck his wrists together, but then whipped them up and socked Dad in the chin instead. Dad fell backward, and Ian gave him a shove, then twisted away and sprinted toward me. Dad lifted the chain, and I held my breath, expecting Ian to trip when he came to the end of it. The chain pulled taut but then slipped out of Ian's shoe, clinking to the pavement. He must have unlocked the cuff and then tucked the chain into his shoe so Dad wouldn't notice.

Ian raced past me and jumped into the still-running sedan, swinging his legs in and slamming the door. Dad reached for his hip and ran forward as Ian peeled out. Ian gave one wave to Dad over his shoulder. I could see his grin in his rearview as he pulled out of the parking lot.

I stared at the car, heart pumping. What would happen now? Dad said no high-speed chases, but Ian had stolen that girl's car. I'd let him run by me; did that make me some kind of accessory to his crime after all? I didn't know much about stealing things, but I knew you didn't want to be around when other people did it.

I looked back at Dad to see if he was worried. He'd know what we could and couldn't get in trouble for.

Dad was already jerking the gas hose out of the pump. As he leapt for the cab, his hand went to his pocket. He patted one pocket, then the other, and then jumped out of the truck to check the back ones. He swore, reaching for the ignition and checking the crack in the seat, but came up with nothing.

"Son of a bitch stole my keys," Dad said.

That must be how he got the cuff unlocked. He

probably grabbed the keys from Dad's pocket before he went in.

"So we're stuck here?" I asked.

Dad shook his head, holding out his hand. "Not unless you've lost your set."

"All I've got is the trailer key."

"There's a spare truck key in the back."

I handed Dad my key, and he opened the trailer door, then handed it back to me.

Ian had seen his chance, and he'd taken it. Now he was gone, and I was still stuck here with Dad, no better off than I had been before.

That's when the girl in the UW sweatshirt came out of the station, her hair pulled into a ponytail. She gaped at the place where the car had been, and then looked around the parking lot at the other cars.

"What the hell?" she asked, looking at Dad. "Where's my car?"

Dad looked at the empty space where the car had been, and then at the road where Ian had pulled away. He sighed.

I hopped up into the truck and sat back on the bench seat, feeling my heart rate begin to slow. I could tell what Dad was thinking. We weren't going to catch him, even if Dad had been up to the chase.

Still, that would have been a good story to tell Jamie—the kind of story he wanted to hear about my exciting new life.

Jamie. My face flushed as I thought about Ian, and the way I'd liked having his breath on my neck and his knees pressed against my back. Mom always said that cheating was bad karma, and even if I wasn't technically cheating, I really didn't want to risk it. I'd have to send him an extra-long e-mail next time I got to a library to make up for it.

Cheyenne, Wyoming.
Minutes since Ian ran: 1.
Distance from Salt Lake City, Utah: 441.44 miles.

7

The girl in the sweatshirt swore, reached for her pocket, and swore again. She looked over at Dad. "Someone stole my car."

"Yup," Dad said. He reached for his pocket and pulled out his ID. "I'm a bail enforcement agent, and that man who took your car escaped from my custody."

I looked back at Dad. Couldn't he get in trouble for admitting that?

"The more information you can give me about your car, the better the chances are that I can find him, and it."

She wrinkled her eyes at him, looking at his ID. "So, you're a cop?"

"No," Dad said. "I'm a bail enforcement agent."

She cocked her head at him, like she didn't have a clue what he was talking about. "He's a bounty hunter," I said from the cab.

The girl's eyes widened, and Dad shot me a shut-up look.

"Think of me as a private investigator," Dad said. "I'm chasing the guy who took your car, so I'll probably find the car in the process. Any information you can give me will make you that much more likely to get your car back."

"I think I should call the police," she said.

"Yes, you should. But the cops have a million other things to do, so unless someone calls in an abandoned vehicle or the thief breaks some other laws, they aren't likely to find it in any kind of hurry. That's where I come in." He held out his hand to shake hers. "I'm Robert Maxwell. What's your name?"

"Caroline," she said, hesitantly accepting his hand.

Dad reached for his clipboard and pulled a certificate and a business card out of the papers at the back. "This is my Colorado license," he said, "and the card of the bondsman I work for. You can call him, and he'll verify who I am. It's my job to bring that punk in to the police, and I'm happy to help you get your car back in the process, if you're willing to share some information with me."

Caroline reached for her pocket and then closed her eyes. "My wallet was in the car. I was just coming out to get it. That means he has . . ."

"Your whole life in his hands," Dad said, his tone softening. "But that gives us more ways to find him." Dad handed her his cell phone. "You call the cops and make your report. And when you're done with that, you can call Cal to check up on me if you'd like. After that, I'd appreciate it if you'd share your license plate number with me, and anything else I might be able to trace to find him."

Caroline looked Dad up and down. "You're really a bounty hunter?" she asked. "Like Big Mike? You don't look much like one."

"That's what I keep saying," I said.

Dad chuckled. "Something like that. I'll be right here when you're done with that call."

When Caroline walked off a couple of feet to make her call, he shook his head at me. "Don't use those words with people," he said. "Gives them all kinds of misconceptions."

"Okay. Sorry. I didn't know you had to have a license."

"Depends on the state. I'm registered in the ones that require it. Wyoming doesn't."

"Isn't Cal going to be upset when he finds out you let Ian steal that car?"

"Things go wrong on the job," Dad said. "Cal knows that. He trusts me to deal with it."

Dad went to pick up his chain and cuff and stowed them in the trailer. When he came back to the truck he picked up his clipboard and started scribbling notes on it. He looked over his shoulder at Caroline, who stood by the gas pump, talking on his cell phone. Dad swore again.

"Still, I can't believe I let him get my keys," he said. "So stupid."

I felt a stab of guilt for not doing something to stop Ian. I'd stood there like an idiot while he took a poor girl's car. So much for showing Dad I could be helpful.

Sitting in the cab, I could almost smell him in the stale air. I didn't have to let him go. I could have intercepted him. In my mind I pictured myself stepping into his way, his body crashing into mine, stumbling, and knocking us both over onto the concrete. His breath puffed against my face as I looked up into his eyes, and then he smiled.

I turned my head in the direction of Dad's clipboard, snapping myself out of it.

"Do you think you can find him again?" I asked.

"Sure," Dad said. "It's not like he's been such a genius at hiding. It's just going to take a while longer, now that he knows who's coming for him."

When Caroline came back with the cell phone, she

leaned against the side of the truck. "The police say I'm not obligated to share any information with you," she said.

"They're right," Dad said. "But did they give you odds on finding your car today?"

Caroline sighed. "Look, I live in Laramie. If I give you the information on my car, could you give me a ride home?"

"Sure," Dad said. "Hop in."

"But you should know I called my roommate and gave her your license plate number."

Dad smiled. "That was probably smart."

"I already got my car stolen today," she said. "I don't need to get kidnapped, too."

Dad opened the truck door for her, and she climbed into the back seat. As she sat down, she eyed the bolt and chain on the floor but didn't comment.

"So," Dad said as he started the engine. "Tell us everything you can about the car and the wallet. Make, model, year, credit card numbers, driver's license numbers, everything."

Caroline was quiet for a moment. "My credit card numbers, huh? How's that going to help?"

"This guy's a thief, right?"

"Apparently." Caroline still sounded confused. I smiled back at her, trying to look comforting.

"So he's likely to use those cards," Dad said. "I can track them if he does, and use that information to find him."

"You can track someone else's card numbers?"

"That's my job."

Caroline passed Dad's bounty-hunting license over the seat, and I took it. As I leafed through Dad's clipboard to put it away, I came across a mug shot of Ian. His physical description was printed under it, as well as his former addresses. At the bottom of the page, someone had written, "Charges that didn't stick," followed by a string of abbreviations.

"I'll take that back now," Dad said, grabbing the clipboard from me before I could decipher them.

"You don't have to give me any information you don't want to," Dad said to Caroline. "It's up to you. I'll give you the ride either way, but if you don't tell me anything, it'll be a while before you see that car again."

Dad handed his cell phone to Caroline again. "You also might want to call the credit card companies," he said. "Tell them to put a watch on your cards."

Dad handed me his clipboard and pulled onto I-80 in the direction of Laramie.

The first call Caroline made was to her roommate again, to check the license plate information on her registration and the credit card numbers from her old statements. She still hesitated with the card information, but then she read it off to me, letting me take it all down. By the time we reached Laramie, she'd reported all her cards stolen, and I'd noted a pretty extensive list of data. I sat up a little taller in my seat. It felt good to actually contribute to Dad's business for once, instead of tagging along. Maybe, in some small way, it made up for how I'd taunted him with Ian.

"This is good," Dad said. "Shouldn't take more than a day or so for us to find him."

"Thanks," Caroline said. "I really appreciate that."

"Thank *you*," Dad said. "Trust me, this helps us both."

We dropped Caroline off at her dorm, and Dad stopped at the university library so I could upload my non-existent homework while he called around to get reports on Caroline's car and credit cards.

With no homework to upload, I went directly to my e-mail. Maybe Mom had contacted me. Maybe I'd finally get to know where she was.

I had one new e-mail. From Anna. At least that was something.

The library computer took forever to load, and I bounced up and down in my chair a little, waiting for the words to pop onto the screen.

Gonorrhea is on standby, Anna wrote. **Investigation in progress re: his jerkiness. Love you.**

I smiled. Anna was probably following Jamie through the hallways, quizzing everyone he breathed at. She never did anything halfway.

That was it on the e-mail—nothing from Mom, nothing from Jamie, not even any spam. I sighed. My old life dwindled away, one piece at a time. Meanwhile, where was Mom that she couldn't even get to a computer? I couldn't exactly be mad at her when she might be tied up in a basement somewhere.

I rubbed my eyes. Sometimes all those news stories poisoned my brain. I had to stop reading about kidnappings until I knew where Mom was.

Instead I pulled up my blog and logged in. Maybe I'd get an e-mail from Jamie if I gave him a reason to be jealous. I could sure find a story now.

Dad picked up a particularly dangerous skip this morning. We'll call him the Bull. I could tell that he was a force of nature—wild and untamed. His eyes looked right through me, like he could see into my soul.

I rolled my eyes and deleted the last clause. This was getting dangerously close to emo. Ian must have addled my brain. Whatever. Now was the time to set objectivity aside and make Jamie's eyes burn.

**His eyes looked right through me, but there was
also a soft sexiness about him. I interviewed him
twice but couldn't get him to break.**

"Interviewed" might be a stretch, but it's what a
reporter would say, even if she was just talking to a
person on the street.

**As we stopped for gas, the Bull pretended he needed
to pee and then made a break for it, stealing a car
right in front of us. His tires squealed as he sped
out of the parking lot, smiling, and was gone.**

This was the part where I needed to describe the
high-speed chase—the one Dad refused to have. Oh
well.

The hunt begins again.

I wondered if it would work. By this point I'd be
happy to receive any kind of message, even an angry one.
Mom always said a jealous boyfriend was an attentive
boyfriend.

I posted the entry and logged off.

Dad picked me up a few minutes later, pulling the
trailer into the fire lane along the front of the building. I

expected him to gun it out to go look for Ian, but instead he left the engine idling.

"We need to talk," he said.

My heart pounded. "Did you hear from Mom?"

He looked surprised. "No, nothing like that. We just need to talk about your behavior."

Crap. After Ian's escape, I'd hoped I was off the hook. "What behavior?"

"I know you hate me dragging you along, but you still need to listen to my instructions."

I kept my eyes on the dash. If I was going to get yelled at, might as well play dumb. Sometimes that worked to get Mom off my back.

"What instructions?"

Dad sighed. "I'm trying to have a conversation with you, Ricki. Would you look at me?"

When I looked up at him, he was gripping the steering wheel with one hand. His brow creased as he looked me in the eye.

"I think I've been unfair to you," he said. "I've treated you like a little kid, so you've been acting like one."

I wanted to protest, but I knew what he meant. I'd been trying my best to do the exact opposite of whatever he asked me, which was five-year-old behavior at best.

"Does that mean you're going to stop yelling at me?"

"I want us to come to an understanding. I know you

want to help me out, and I'm happy for the help, but only if I know I can trust you."

I bit my lip. I hadn't given him much of a reason to trust me. I wasn't sure I trusted him, either. "And do you? Trust me?"

Dad's eyes flicked up at the ceiling, which I took for a big fat no.

"Fine," I said.

"This isn't coming out right," Dad said. "Let's park the trailer, and we can talk about it over dinner."

"More tacos?" I asked.

"There's a diner near the freeway. We can eat some sit-down junk food for a change."

"All right," I said. At least I'd be able to eat a salad that hadn't sat in a plastic container for days.

The diner was right off the exit. The dining area only held about twelve tables, but they had a little salad bar and a dessert counter.

Dad ordered a burger, but I got the salad bar and a cup of soup, since those things are hard to eat in the car. After we'd ordered, Dad put his elbows on the table and looked at me.

"So what's this stuff you're always writing?" he asked. "I know it isn't homework."

I didn't want him making fun of my writing, but if I wanted him to trust me, I had to give him something.

"I'm taking notes," I said. "For my blog."

Dad raised his eyebrows. "You write about my work on your blog?"

"Don't worry," I said quickly. "I don't use any names, and I change the details. I don't want to get you in trouble."

Dad nodded. "I'm impressed you thought about that."

"We learned in journalism class about protecting our sources. I figure it goes double since you're my dad."

"You're taking journalism in school?"

"I was before Mom left. That's what I want to do when I'm older."

"That's a good job, and you're good at asking questions. We'll have to see if there's a homeschool course for it."

I'd thought the homeschool courses only came in boring subjects. "That would be cool," I said.

"Journalism can be dangerous, though," Dad said. "Depending on the kind of reporting you're doing, you can end up in some scary situations."

"Like your job," I said. "I bet I could learn a lot from you, if you'd let me."

He actually seemed to consider the idea. "Maybe. But you'll need more training than I can give you. Journalists need a college education, and that means you need to focus on your homework."

"Not all journalism is for newspapers," I said. "I want to be a blogger."

"That doesn't sound very stable."

"Kind of like your job."

Dad laughed. "Is that your answer for everything?"

"Only because it's true."

"I suppose it is. Look, since you're riding along, there are some things about my job you need to understand. Ian isn't your schoolmate. He's a criminal, and probably a dangerous one. You can't go making eyes at him like he's your boyfriend."

Too bad Jamie wasn't here to hear that. "We were just talking. That doesn't make him my boyfriend."

"I know that. You're a smart girl. You've got a lot going for you. I like this idea of you becoming a journalist. You've got the wits to be good at it, and you're stubborn enough to succeed. You could travel all over the world doing that. But guys like Ian will just manipulate you. They'll take you places you don't want to be. So I want you to steer clear, you understand?"

I was quiet for a moment. Dad was treating my journalism plans like they were a good idea, and I didn't want to ruin that. "I get it," I said.

"I'll make you a deal," he said. "From now on, you do what I ask of you. And in return I'll keep you in the loop about my leads, and I'll let you keep an eye on the skips when they're chained in the truck. I'm still not going to take you in when I'm cornering them, but once they're cuffed and chained you can help. Maybe you can learn something about tracking leads that will be useful to you later. But you've got to keep your head on straight and be more careful. No more flirting with fugitives, okay?"

I leaned back in my seat. I hadn't really expected Dad to be so reasonable. It would be nice to be able to help out—I'd end up with some great stories.

"It's a deal," I said.

Dad's burger came, and I fixed a salad at the bar filled with green peppers and mushrooms drowned in vinaigrette. When I got back to the table, Dad had slathered his French fries with honey-mustard sauce.

"I'm worried about Mom," I said. I had to be careful here. I didn't want him going back on our deal, but we needed to talk about this while he was still being reasonable.

"I'm sorry," Dad said. "I wish she wouldn't worry you like this."

"Bad things happen to people sometimes," I said. "What if she's hurt somewhere, and we're not even looking for her?"

Dad thought about that for a second, which was an improvement at least. "Look," he said, "we don't have any leads on where she is. She's an adult, and she's left like this before."

"Never for this long."

"No," Dad said, "but all signs point to her being fine. She'll contact you when she's ready. Until then, you keep your mind on your homework and on helping me, okay?"

I took a big bite of my salad and chewed. He might be reasonable now, but it didn't change that he'd left me alone with Mom for most of my life, and he wasn't really listening to what I needed now. I kept shoveling salad into my mouth, to keep myself from asking the unaskable question: If I'd run off instead of Mom, would he come looking for me?

8

As we drove to a trailer park for the night, Dad pulled some papers out of the glove box. "We have a deal, right? You're going to listen, and I'm going to let you help."

"Right," I said.

"Good. Because I traded faxes with Cal at Kinko's while you were at the library. We have another skip to pick up."

"So we're not chasing after Ian?" I'd just told Dad I'd stop flirting with skips. So why did I itch to talk with Ian again?

"Still waiting for those credit reports to come through. Takes time, and if he's smart, he won't even use them. We'll go after him when we get a break. This next one's a breeze, though. He's one of my regulars. Won't take long."

"You have *regulars*?"

Dad grinned. "Just a few. Stan gets picked up on a DUI or a drunk and disorderly every six months or so. This time it's driving without a license, since he hasn't gotten his card back from the last DUI. He forgets his court dates. Wanders off."

"So where do we look?" I asked. "His apartment?"

"Nah. Cal already checked there, and he's pretty sure Stan's been gone for a while. His mail has piled up. He lands at his mom's place in Kearney about half the time, so we can start there in the morning."

"Are you sure it can wait until then?"

"Has to. If I work tired, I work sloppy."

"It's only five o'clock."

"Add a five-hour drive to Kearney and it'll be ten. After tracking Stan down I'll be too tired to haul him back, and I sure don't want to share my bed with him. If he's at his mom's, he'll still be there tomorrow. Besides, that'll give our friend Ian some time to make use of those credit cards."

"Isn't it wrong for you to hope he breaks the law?"

"I'm not hoping. Just being practical."

"Sounds like hope to me."

Dad smiled. "Well, maybe a little."

We camped at a motor-home park in Cheyenne. I spent most of the night listening to the wind whistle against the weather stripping on the window above my head. The cold air crept in, wrapping around my neck. I pulled the blankets tighter. They smelled of dust.

If Mom didn't come back, that's what would become of the old me. Dust and memory ghosts. Being on the road with Dad was starting to feel like the new normal, but the more normal this became, the more my old life was fading away. And this life could end just as easily—easier even, since Dad didn't have a great track record of wanting me around. I squeezed my eyes tight, trying to block out the thought. Then I thought of Ian, staring me straight in the eyes, only the chains keeping him from reaching out to me.

In the morning, when we headed out, I flipped open my notebook and wrote, *Kearney, Nebraska. Looking for Dad's regular. Wanted for DUI.* Dad bought us some doughnuts at the gas station, and off we went.

Once we got on the freeway, Dad picked up his cell phone and Velcroed it to the dash, hitting the voice-dial button.

"Name?" the phone said.

"Margaret Kentworth."

"Dialing."

The phone began to ring, and a woman's voice came over the speaker—low and gruff. "Yeah?"

"Margaret," Dad said. "Robert Maxwell here. I'm looking for Stan. You seen him?"

"Hell yes," the voice said. "He's sitting out back. You coming to get him?"

"Sure am," Dad said. "Be there in five hours or so."

"He'll probably be at the bar by then, 'less he's out of money. You know the one?"

"Yeah, I know. Thanks, ma'am."

"You bet. Treat Stanley nice, now."

"Always do."

"Yes, I know. Bye, now."

Dad hit the off button on the phone and smiled at me. "See? Piece of cake."

Raindrops splattered the windshield, and I squinted at Dad.

"You called up his mother to tell her we're coming?"

"Sure. That way I know we're headed in the right direction. She's out of town a lot, though, visiting grand-kids and such. Sometimes I have to make the drive up anyway."

"Why would she sell out her son like that?"

"She hates the way Stan lives his life, but she can't bear to turn him in herself. Good woman, she is."

"I'm not sure any woman who turns in her own son is all that good."

"She does what she thinks is right. I happen to agree with her."

"Seems pretty warped to me."

Under the name of the city in my notebook I wrote, *Stan Kentworth. Turned in by his own mother.*

"You working on a blog post?" Dad asked.

"Yeah," I said.

"You just keep remembering to change all the identifying information, okay?"

I closed the notebook and shoved it under my leg. "I was doing that before you asked."

"I know. Maybe eventually we can get you a laptop, so you could work on that no matter where you are."

I didn't know what to say to that. Laptops were expensive. "That'd be nice," I said. "Thanks."

The clock above the rearview mirror said it was nine, which meant that Jamie would be wandering out to his locker between classes. Meeting me, if I was there. Who was he meeting now? Shelby? Maren?

I smiled, thinking of Anna spying on him. Thank goodness for her. She'd find out what was really going on.

"Can I use the phone next time we stop?" I asked.

"Sure," Dad said. "You want to call your grandma?"

"No," I said. "Just a friend."

"Okay," Dad said, "you can use the phone, but tell your friends not to call it all the time. It's still a business number."

The drive to Kearney was long, so I buckled down on my algebra homework and actually made some progress through conic sections. Even so, I couldn't do math for more than an hour straight without feeling like my eyes were starting to bleed. Eventually I had to get Dad talking again.

"So, has a skip ever run from you before?" I asked.

"Skips are always running from me. It's my job to chase them."

"No, I mean after you caught him, like Ian did."

"Ah. I've had some skips try to get away, sure. Some of them break and run, even though they have nowhere to go, just to make me wrestle them back into the truck. I think sometimes they do it to make my job harder. But none of them have ever stolen a car after I picked them up."

"Why didn't you shoot Ian when he got in the car?"

"At a gas station? What if I'd shot a bystander?"

"Aren't you a better shot than that?"

"Don't believe everything you see in the movies. It's hard to hit a guy with a handgun while he's driving away in a car. Besides, I could get my concealed carry taken away for that. Wasn't worth the risk."

"But you do carry a gun on you?"

"Sure," Dad said. "You hadn't noticed?"

"I guess I wouldn't know what to look for. I've rarely even seen a real gun."

Dad glanced over at me. "You've never shot one?"

"When would I have done that? It's not like Mom's a gun fanatic."

"She was a pretty good shot, back in the day."

"Mom shot a gun?"

"I used to take her shooting every now and again."

That was a strange image—Mom and Dad going shooting together. In fact, it was hard to imagine them doing just about anything together.

"Huh," I said. "Go figure."

Dad smiled. "Would you like to try it?"

"Shooting?"

"Sure."

The idea of holding a gun in my hands scared me a little. I guess I'd been scarred by all those TV shows about kids shooting each other when they're playing around with their parents' guns.

"Maybe sometime."

"How about now?"

I looked around at the flat expanse of middle-of-nowhere Nebraska. "Here?"

"Sure. If you want."

"Aren't you in a hurry?"

"I haven't heard back about Ian yet, and Stan's not going anywhere. I think we can spare twenty minutes."

"But you're always talking about keeping me out of danger. Now you want to hand me a gun?"

Dad laughed. "I'll teach you gun safety. I used to go hunting with my dad when I was younger than you. You can handle it."

The idea that Dad would rather arm his daughter than let her talk to a skip seemed a little backward to me, but I had to admit I was curious about what it would feel like to shoot his gun. I'd been asking for more responsibility, and teaching me to shoot was a good step. If I could do it well, maybe Dad would be impressed.

"Yeah," I said. "Okay."

Dad waited for a turnoff long enough to fit the trailer and then pulled over. He climbed out to unlock the security boxes on the side of the pickup.

"I thought you kept your gun on you," I said.

Dad reached for his belt and pulled out a pistol, keeping it pointed at the ground. "I'm just getting some ammo. Don't keep a lot on me. I don't get shot at much."

"Much?"

Dad just smiled, pulling a cartridge out of the bottom of the handle and loading it with bullets. I usually thought of guns as having round barrels, but this one was rectangular with a round hole running through it. The whole thing was made out of a dark gray metal.

"Safety's on," he said, handing me the gun and showing me how to hold it. "But keep it pointed at the ground while you're carrying it. Take it slow, and make sure to never point it at anything you don't want to shoot. Keep your finger out of the action and away from the trigger until you're all aimed and ready to fire."

For once, I didn't object to any of Dad's rules. I kept my eyes on the barrel, making sure it pointed at the dust, where it wouldn't do much damage if it fired. The gun was heavier than I expected it to be. I wondered how anyone held them steady.

"You don't need to be so stiff. Just be careful with it, is all."

"But you just said—"

"The gun's just a tool. The danger is in what you do with it. Just don't point it at anything living, all right? Or at the truck. Especially the tires."

I nodded before I realized he was making fun of me.

Dad ducked into the trailer, and I looked back at the highway, expecting any minute for some cop to show up and see me standing there holding a gun. What would I do if he told me to drop my weapon? Dropping a loaded gun didn't sound like the safest move.

Dad came back carrying three empty soda cans. "Come on," he said, walking around the trailer so it obscured us from the road.

Scrubby weeds covered the land stretching away from the turnoff. I kept the gun pointed at the ground as Dad walked out a ways and set the cans on a rock. Then he came back to me, taking my gun hand in his and helping me to lift it.

"Hold it with both hands," Dad said, fitting my other hand onto my wrist to brace it. "Keep your elbows locked. The gun's going to kick, which will hurt your aim."

"Don't guns hurt when they kick?"

"That's shotguns. The handle on a shotgun hits you right here." He patted me on the shoulder. "But this is a handgun, so you don't need to worry about that."

I was glad to start out with something pain free.

"Here's the safety," Dad said, clicking it off before I could really see what he was doing. "Now you're ready to go. Aim at the cans and squeeze the trigger."

My arm was starting to shake, mostly from the weight. I wasn't sure how long I could hold it out like that, so I pointed toward the cans and squeezed.

Dad should have warned me about the noise. The bang was so loud it deafened me, leaving an eerie silence.

"How was it?" Dad asked when I could hear again.

"Um, okay," I said, looking at the three cans still sitting there in a row. "I didn't hit anything."

Dad laughed. "It's all right. Go ahead and empty the clip."

I tried to aim better this time, then squeezed the trigger, letting the rest of the bullets go. The gun kicked with each shot, making my wrists give this involuntary little flick, like when the doctor hits your knee with a hammer. I must have been holding my breath, because when the bullets were gone I gasped, adrenaline pouring through me. When I finished, the cans all still sat there. I hadn't managed to hit a single one.

"That's actually kind of fun," I said. "Even if I suck."

Dad clapped me on the shoulder. "Glad you like it. Next time maybe we'll work on your aim. Don't feel bad, though. Handguns are rough. Maybe I'll take you to a range sometime. Let you try a rifle."

I was almost sorry when Dad took the gun and packed it back in the security box. I would have been all the way sorry if I wasn't shaking, and not just from the weight of the gun.

"Thanks," I said, climbing into the cab.

"No problem."

That's when it occurred to me that I hadn't thanked Dad for much over the last week.

"Really," I said. "Thank you."

"Sure. At the very least it's something to brag to your boyfriend about when you get back to Utah."

"How'd you know I have a boyfriend?"

"You said so on the phone with your friend."

"Oh," I said. I'd forgotten about that.

"I'd figured you had one before that, being as anxious to get back to your grandma's as you were."

"Oh." Maybe he wasn't going to be a total freak about it after all.

"Besides, you're a pretty girl. No reason you shouldn't have a boyfriend, even if you are a little young."

"I've had boyfriends since I was twelve."

"Twelve? Did your mom know about that?"

"She used to drive me to the mall to meet guys all the time, before I started dating guys with cars."

"Huh," Dad said. "I guess that was her call." He didn't look too pleased.

I almost made a snotty comment about how Dad couldn't decide since he wasn't around, but I caught myself.

"So, does your mom date much?"

That was kind of a weird thing for him to ask. "Yeah. Why?"

"Just wondering. Did she bring guys home?"

"Sure. And a couple of her boyfriends lived with us for a while." I'd even liked a few, but none of them had ever been around long enough to be dadlike. The ones who thought they could boss me around lasted even less time than the rest.

"How did you feel about that?"

Now Dad was probing, trying to find reasons why Mom was a bad parent. "Okay, I guess. Some of them made Mom happy, so that was nice."

"Some of them."

"Yeah, some of them. What about you? Who's your girlfriend?"

"What makes you think I have one?"

"You must be having these personal meetings with someone."

Dad was quiet for a second. "Nope," he said. "No girlfriend. If I had one, you'd have met her by now."

For some reason I felt relieved. "I guess it would be hard to have a relationship when you're traveling around all the time."

Dad nodded. "That's one of the reasons I got into bounty hunting in the first place. If I traveled around a lot, I didn't have to get involved with anybody."

"I don't think that's supposed to be a perk."

"Don't be so sure."

"Seriously. Who chooses a job so they don't have to date? Couldn't you work at a desk and just say no to girls?"

"I suppose I could take the Nancy Reagan approach."

"Who?"

"Nancy Reagan? Just say no?"

I gave him a blank look.

"Never mind. The alone time is only one of the things I like about this job."

I couldn't imagine wanting to be alone all the time. But if Dad liked it, how long before he got tired of having me around? "I still think that sounds like a lousy way to live."

"Yeah, I do too. Now."

"You said you liked your job."

"I do, but I'm starting to think about the things I've been missing."

Like me? I wanted to ask. But instead I said, "What changed?"

Dad smiled, but he didn't respond. I hated it when he did that. I was hoping what changed was having me along, but I'd feel pretty stupid if I said that and it turned out not to be true.

Kearney, Nebraska.
Days since Mom left: 31.
Distance from Salt Lake City: 755.1 miles.

9

I put my notebook inside my algebra book and wrote down everything I could remember about shooting Dad's gun. I got so involved in the writing, I was actually surprised to look up and see we were in Kearney.

"Want me to drop you somewhere?" Dad asked. "You can get a bite to eat and make that phone call."

"I thought you said you were going to let me be more involved."

"Did I not tell you all the details about Stan's case? I'll even let you babysit him after I've got him in the truck. Stan's not too dangerous, but I'm still not taking you into the bar while I drag him out. You're underage. There are laws."

"Fine. I'll wait in the car."

"Suit yourself."

We pulled into a slummy commercial district, past a couple of liquor stores and an "adult" bookstore, its window curtained behind glowing triple Xs.

Dad parked on the street and motioned toward a bar across the way. "If Stan's still here, he's probably pretty drunk. This could take a few minutes."

"Sure," I said as Dad climbed out of the car. Sprinkles of rain hit the windshield again, and a blast of cold air swept in. Dad slammed the door and walked into the bar.

I picked up my algebra book again, but a man wearing a heavy coat and tattered jeans walked past my window. He turned around, making eyes at me. I looked down at my book, trying to ignore him, until he walked up and rapped on the glass.

I jumped. His face was so close to my window that it fogged the glass. Raindrops slipped through the grease in his hair.

I clicked the lock on the door. "Go away," I said through the glass.

The man made a pouty face at me, but then he walked past the trailer and out of sight.

I held my breath, watching in the mirror until he disappeared around the corner. Then I pushed open the truck door and headed toward the bar. I didn't want to wreck things with Dad, but he couldn't expect me to wait in the car in a neighborhood like this. The bar might be full of creeps, but at least Dad would be there to protect me.

The bar reeked of alcohol and too much skin stuck to the vinyl stools and booths. I wanted to take a can of Lysol and drench the place.

The room was pretty much empty, so I found Dad right away, sitting on the edge of a stool next to a hunched-over man wearing a green slicker and a pair of black rain boots.

"Come on, Stan," Dad said. "Don't make this difficult."

Dad's arms hung loose at his sides, and he leaned back on the stool. This wasn't even beginning to be difficult, and he knew it.

"Buy me one more?" Stan said. "Then I'll come along quiet."

As I approached, Dad gave me a hard look over Stan's shoulder. I mouthed "sorry" at him and then sat down in a booth by the far wall. Hopefully Dad would give me the chance to explain before he got all pissed.

The only other people in the bar were the bartender and a couple in the corner. It was only two o'clock, so the bar probably hadn't even been open that long. I expected the bartender to get mad and kick me out for being underage, but he barely glanced at me.

From this angle I could see Stan's face. Stubble grew over his large chin. Between that and his angular nose, he would have looked a lot like a Disney villain if it weren't for his wide grin.

"No more drinks," Dad said. "You can't have them in the car, and we've got to get a move on."

"Besides," the bartender called over, "I told you no more."

Two o'clock was pretty early to be cut off. Plus, Stan didn't look all that drunk—drunk people were supposed to lisp and tilt and drool. That's what Shelby did at that party last spring when her boyfriend got her wasted. But Stan just sat on his stool, grinning at Dad and shaking his head.

"See? I've been cut off. You wouldn't want to take me to jail sober, would you?"

Dad shook his head. "Something tells me you're not completely sober yet, Stan. Maybe the nice people at the jail will buy you some beer."

Stan laughed a deep belly laugh, and Dad smiled, standing up from the stool. "Come on," Dad said. "My daughter's waiting."

Stan's grin widened. "You got your daughter with you? I never knew you had a daughter."

I looked down at the table. I knew it was stupid to be

mad about that. Stan was a skip—he probably didn't know a lot of things about Dad's life. But I still couldn't help feeling like I hardly existed.

Dad helped Stan off his stool and steered him toward the door. He looked over at me, jerking his head for me to follow, and Stan traced his gaze.

"This is her?" he asked, walking over to me. "This is your little girl?"

"I'm not so little," I said.

Dad shook his head at me, and Stan laughed again. "No, you aren't, are you? You're a right pretty little thing."

"Again with the little."

"Come on," Dad said. "Let's go." The bartender nodded at Dad as we ambled outside to the truck.

Dad didn't say anything to criticize me about coming into the bar, probably because he didn't want to seem weak in front of his skip. He stuck Stan in the back seat behind me, but he didn't cuff him or chain his feet to the floor.

After Dad loaded Stan into the truck, I walked him around to the driver's side. If I explained myself before Dad brought it up, maybe I could head off the fight before it even started.

"I didn't mean to come in," I said.

"Did someone drag you.?"

"Well, no. But there was this creepy guy knocking on my window, and I got scared."

Dad looked at me for a second. "All right, then. I'll overlook it."

I climbed into my seat. Dad started the engine and drove the truck toward the freeway.

"You can turn here," Stan said as we passed a residential neighborhood. "My mom's place is just down the street."

"I'm not taking you to your mother's, Stan. You know that."

"Just thought I'd save you the trouble of the drive," Stan said. "Drop me off, and I promise to stay out of trouble."

"You can't stay out of something you're already in. If you want to save me the trouble, you should show up in court when you're supposed to."

"Damn dates. Can't seem to remember 'em."

"Maybe you should get a date book."

"Had one. Lost it."

"A watch, then," I said. "A fancy one that remembers appointments and beeps if you forget."

Stan laughed again. "Smart girl you've got, Max."

Dad rolled his eyes. "Tell me about it," he said.

I frowned at him. I couldn't tell if he was making fun of me or not. I didn't really get called smart a whole lot. Smart kids got As. I slid by with Cs. Besides, Mom said it was more important to be clever than smart.

As we returned to the freeway, Stan talked nonstop about why Dad should just drop him off, and how he didn't deserve to be in court anyway. He sold his point so hard, I wondered if Dad should have chained him, but when I looked over my shoulder I found Stan relaxed against the seat, grinning broadly.

While Stan jabbered, Dad picked up his cell phone and punched some buttons. "Hang on, Stan," Dad said, waving the phone. "I need to return a call." He held the phone with his shoulder and handed me his clipboard. "Take notes for me, would you?"

Dad took the phone from his ear, pushed another button, and then returned it. "Hey, Joe, this is Max. Do you have anything on those credit cards?"

He threw the phone onto speaker so I could hear the voice on the other end.

"Sure," Joe said. "Someone tried to use the card a couple of hours ago, at the Ramada in North Platte."

Dad grinned wide.

I wrote, *Ramada. North Platte.*

"Thanks, Joe."

"Anytime, Max. Hey, give me a call next time you're in town. We'll catch a Rockies game or something."

"Will do. See you later." Dad hung up the phone.

"North Platte's on our route back to Denver," Dad said. "We can stop on the way."

"Where're you taking me?" Stan asked.

"Just to check on some business," Dad said. "You don't mind, do you, Stan?"

"Oh, no," Stan said. "In fact, I could ride with you for a bit longer than that if you want. 'Specially if we can stop at a 7-Eleven."

Dad rolled his eyes, looking over at me. "I'll bribe a clerk to tell me which room he's in. If he's there, I can drag him out no problem. If he's not, sometimes these things take a while." He winked sidelong at me and then raised his voice to talk to Stan again.

"Do you think you can babysit my daughter for me?" he asked. "I shouldn't be too long."

Stan laughed. "Doesn't seem like she needs much baby-sitting."

"Oh, you know how it is. Guess I'm overprotective. Could you look out for her?"

"Sure," Stan said.

Dad gave me a nod. He was going to make good on his promise to let me watch Stan, even though I'd gone into the bar when he told me not to.

I winked back at Dad. "I don't need a babysitter."

"Come on, honey," Stan said. "I'm not so bad. I'll buy you a drink."

"You'll both stay in the truck," Dad said. "I don't want my daughter going with you to buy booze."

"I was kidding, Max. You know me. Always a joker."

Stan launched into a story about the days when he used to babysit his little sister when he was in high school. He rambled the rest of the way to North Platte, and Dad smiled so much that he didn't ask about my homework once.

The Ramada wasn't hard to find once we pulled off the freeway; it was taller than just about everything else in town. Dad parked down the street from it. He pulled a pair of binoculars out from under his seat and peered up at the hotel windows.

"Didn't know you were such a peeping Tom, Max," Stan said.

"You know how it is," Dad said. "I take what I can get."

"You're not likely to find him by looking at the hotel, are you?" I asked.

"I'm checking the windows. Skips are always looking out the windows, especially when they know they're being followed."

"Well? Do you see him?"

Dad shook his head. "Sheers are drawn in some of the rooms, though. That means they can see out and I can't see in."

The sun cast a golden glare on the building, adding shine to some of the windows. That probably didn't help.

Dad sighed. "Time to go hassle the clerk. You watch Ricki for me, okay, Stan?"

Stan saluted, and Dad climbed out of the car. "You be careful," he mouthed at me.

I nodded, and Dad turned and ran down the street to the front doors of the hotel.

North Platte, Nebraska.
Days since Mom left: 31.
Distance from Salt Lake City: 659 miles.

 # 10

S tan stretched his arms over his head until they tapped the ceiling of the truck. Then he rolled down his window and stuck his head out.

"Hey, sweetheart," Stan said to me. "I'm going to take a little walk."

"You're supposed to stay here," I said. "If you go get a drink, who'll look out for me?"

"Well, see, I'm not going to go very far." Stan was already pulling up on the door handle, but the door didn't open. It must have a child lock. I relaxed. That's why Dad hadn't bothered to chain Stan before he left.

I needed to get him talking. "So," I said, "you have a girlfriend, Stan?"

"I got me some lady friends. Don't like to stick to just one, though."

"Why's that?"

"I'm too much man to settle down."

"Sure you just can't get a woman to keep you?"

"Have you had a look at me?" Stan asked, motioning to his chest. His shirt collar was tattered at the seams, and his shirt looked to be two sizes too big.

"Do you have a job?" I asked.

"Not often."

Listening to this was depressing. "Do you think maybe you should get one?" I asked.

Stan shrugged. "I get one now and again. They don't last too long, though."

"You forget to show up?"

"Forget to show up sober, anyway."

That surprised me. I hadn't realized Stan knew he was a drunk.

"People have got all these rules," he continued. "You know how it is."

I thought of Dad and his obsession with the law. Maybe he kept all those rules because he was afraid of turning out like this—like a skip.

"I'll be going now," Stan said, rising in his seat. His shoulders hunched over against the ceiling.

"I'd really like you to stay," I said. "This neighborhood scares me." I looked around. We were in a pretty nice section of town—no reason to be scared here.

Instead of arguing with me, Stan rolled over the back of Dad's seat and landed on the bench on his hands and knees. He pushed open Dad's door, almost nicking the mirror of a passing car. The car honked and sped off down the road, but Stan climbed out into the street anyway without looking. I cringed, expecting the next car to run him right over, but instead he shut the truck door again and disappeared behind the trailer.

"Hey, where are you going?" I asked. "My dad's going to be mad."

"Don't worry, honey. I'll be right back."

I sighed. Dad couldn't possibly expect me to wrestle Stan into the back seat.

I leaned out the window, watching Stan as he ambled toward a strip mall across the street. At the end, next to an aquarium store, sat a dimly lit bar. No big surprise there. Still, the contrast of Stan's dim form against the neon liquor lights looked sad. I wondered how he came to be this way, wandering around, happy to be at a bar and not really aware of anything else in his life. Dad might be half a loser, but seeing a whole loser really put things in perspective.

I sighed as Stan swung the door open and stepped

inside. Most I could do now was try to coax him back before Dad returned to find us both gone.

I grabbed Dad's clipboard and scribbled him a note with an arrow pointing toward the bar, and then opened the door and hopped out of the truck.

This bar had more people in it, probably because it was nearing evening. A wiry guy in one of the booths looked up at me. He was wearing a camo shirt, rolled up at the sleeves to reveal a network of spider-web tattoos running up the inside of his arms. He flashed me a crooked smile. "Hey, sweetheart," he said, "can I buy you a drink?"

I walked quickly away from the booth. Mom said that it was better to ignore creeps when they tried to hit on you, because actually talking to them just gave them the attention they wanted.

Stan had already settled himself on a stool.

This room had the same smell as the last bar—the reek of bodies mixed with the tang of alcohol. I knew Mom went to bars sometimes, but now, having been in two in one day, I couldn't imagine the appeal.

"Hey," I said. "Why don't you get a drink and bring it back to the car?"

"Nah," Stan said. "Half the fun is sitting and talking. Why don't you take a seat?"

I could see the bartender wiping down the other end of the bar, already giving me the evil eye.

"I don't think I'm allowed to be in here."

"You're a pretty girl. You can flirt your way in." Stan gave me a big grin, so I thought he might be joking, but I didn't know him well enough to be sure.

The bartender walked over to us. "You lost?" he asked me.

"No," I said. "I'm here for him." I pointed at Stan.

"She's my bounty hunter's daughter," Stan said. "Could you get us each a drink?"

The bartender raised his eyebrows at the news that Stan had himself a bounty hunter, but he didn't comment. "I'll need to see some ID first," he said, looking at me.

I could flash my fake ID. Dad would love that.

The only ID I had besides that was my high school card, which had SOPHOMORE embossed across the top in big blue letters.

"We both need to be getting back to the car," I said, tugging on Stan's sleeve. I hoped he wouldn't take that as permission to touch me.

"My bounty hunter will be looking for me, I expect," he said to the bartender. "Can you get me a beer to go?"

"I'm not serving anyone until I see some ID." He was still looking at me, which was kind of funny, since Stan was the one who'd ordered the beer.

Stan waved at the door. "All right, honey. You better get back and tell your dad where to find me."

"I left him a note," I said.

"Great," the bartender said. "But I'm still going to have to ask you to leave."

"I just got here," Stan said. "Haven't even gotten my first drink."

"Not you. The girl."

"I'll pay for hers."

"Not unless she shows some ID, you won't," the bartender said.

"Fine," I said, nodding at Stan. "I'll wait for you outside." I stepped out the door and leaned against the glass storefront. If I leaned just right, I could see Stan sitting at the bar even through the tinted glass. At least this way he wouldn't disappear while I was supposed to be watching him, and I could also flag down Dad when he returned.

I glanced toward the truck to see if Dad had come back yet, and a wave of cold washed over me. The truck was gone, trailer and all.

North Platte, Nebraska.
Seconds since the truck disappeared: 10.
Distance from Salt Lake City: 659 miles.

11

I stood staring at the place where the truck had been. Dad couldn't have left me here, with no one but Stan. What could have happened to make him drive off like that? Had he gotten a lead and run off chasing Ian? He'd probably be pissed that I wasn't in the truck, but technically I was watching Stan like I was supposed to, so I'd actually done what he asked.

I took a slow breath. What should I do? Dad would be coming back once he caught up with Ian. But how long would that be?

Even if Dad was only gone a few minutes, I was still stuck with the anxiety of waiting, of not knowing. Of living with the slim chance that he wouldn't come back at all.

Right then Dad walked back down the street from the direction he'd come, striding his "I'm in charge" stride.

Heat flushed into my cheeks and stomach. Part of me felt like an eight-year-old kid, wanting to hug him for not taking off without telling me. How messed up was I that him not screwing me over felt like a reason to be grateful? He hadn't left at all, for however short a time. But if he was there, and I was here, and Stan was in the bar, where was the truck?

I looked up at the Ramada. It had to be Ian.

Dad looked over at me, and I thought I saw relief in his face before his features stretched into anger.

"Where the hell is the truck?" he asked.

"I don't know. What did you do with it?"

"What did I do with it? I left you with it, that's what I did. How did Stan manage to get the keys?"

"Stan? He's in the bar. I went in after him, so he wouldn't get away, and when I came back out . . ."

"Shit," Dad said, spitting the word out like the shell of a sunflower seed. He kicked at the asphalt. He'd come to the same conclusion I had.

"Ian," I said.

"Ian." Dad walked over to where the truck and trailer had been, kicking at something next to the curb. As I walked closer, I could see it was the clipboard—the one with the note I'd left on the dash for Dad. More swear words poured from his mouth. Dad didn't usually swear around me.

"What is it?" I asked, walking up to him.

He had his jaw clenched like he was trying to stem the flow of his language. He held my note up for me to see. At the bottom, in scrawled handwriting, was another note.

Been waiting for you, bounty man, it read. **Thanks for the truck.**

Dad's hand went to his pocket, then reached for his forehead, like it couldn't decide where to be.

"Your cell phone was in the truck," I said.

"He must have been watching for us," he said. "He tried to use the card. He figured we'd trace it, so he knew we were coming, and he already had the keys." Dad swore again. "Stan's in the bar?"

"Having a beer."

Dad turned around and stalked toward the bar. "I need to use their phone," he said.

I followed Dad. It was hard to believe that Ian had been right here on the street while I was inside arguing with Stan and the bartender. I wondered if he would have approached us if Stan and I had still been in the truck. Would he have stolen us both away?

The bartender glared as I walked in, but Dad waved him over. "Our truck was stolen," he said. "Can I make a few phone calls?"

The bartender looked surprised, then pulled a cord-less phone out from under the register.

"Thanks," Dad said. "You know of any rental-car places around here?"

"There's a small one in town, over by the Jiffy Lube," he said. "It's a long walk, though. My shift ends in twenty minutes, if you want a ride."

"I'll take it," Dad said. "I'll even pay you for your trouble."

"Keep your money. It's not far out of my way. I can't let her stay, though."

"Is there a library nearby?" Dad asked.

"It's within walking distance. Just around the block."

"Come on, Stan," Dad said. "We'll walk Ricki over to the library, and then we can go for a ride."

"I can sit tight," Stan said. He took a long sip of his beer. "I bummed enough for a couple more. I promise I won't move an inch, except to piss."

"Not a chance." Dad took hold of Stan's arm and helped him to his feet. "I don't need any more trouble today."

As we left the bar, Dad said, "I found Caroline's car in the parking lot of the hotel. I'll call to let her know. At least one of us can get our vehicle back."

Dad and Stan left me at the library and headed back to the bar for that ride. The little algebra I'd done was still in the cab of the truck, but I could at least check my e-mail.

This library was uptight about who used their computers, so I had to give the librarian the whole sob story of how our truck got stolen. Then I had to explain how I lived in a travel trailer, so I didn't have an address to prove residency, but I was as much a resident of this town as I was anywhere. She finally gave me a code to log on, but I think it was only to get me to shut up. She walked around behind me four or five times, probably to make sure I wasn't looking at porn or sending out e-mails about Nigerian princes in need of cash.

I checked my e-mail first thing and even refreshed the page twice, hoping the emptiness of my inbox was some kind of loading mistake.

Still nothing from Mom. Not even a word from Jamie. Guess the jealousy angle wasn't working either.

This was getting ridiculous. I couldn't just sit around waiting for people to contact me. I knew exactly where Jamie was, but I still had no idea what was going on with Mom. Dad said I'd be good at his job, and I'd already learned some things from him. If Dad wasn't going to look for her, I needed to do it myself.

I pulled up the website for her e-mail and started plugging in passwords. I knew some of the likely ones, since I'd logged on to pay our bills before. It took me three tries, but finally the browser loaded her in box.

This was a complete invasion of Mom's privacy, and she'd be pissed if she knew I'd done it, but I'd have plenty of ammunition to defend myself when she found out.

The first e-mails were from me, of course, sitting there unread. Under that were a few unopened e-mails from her coworkers, which meant she hadn't gotten official time off work. That wasn't unusual. Mom sometimes switched jobs just so she could have some vacation time. Below that were several old e-mails from some guy named Denis Longwell.

I opened the most recent Denis e-mail. I'll call you tonight, it said. Can't wait to hear your voice.

I scrolled through the e-mails below. Mom had met Denis on a dating website called More Fish. She'd sent him her phone number the e-mail before, and her chat name before that. Most of their actual correspondence must have been over chat, and then over the phone, because the e-mails didn't tell me much about Denis Longwell.

I pulled up the More Fish website, typing in Mom's e-mail address and her same password. The account loaded right up, and there at the top of her contacts list was Denis's profile: DENIS LONGWELL. RETAIL MANAGER. SAN DIEGO, CA.

His picture was fuzzy and badly lit, probably taken from one of those computer cams. He had dark hair and dark eyes and wasn't balding or fat or anything, but his skin and smile both looked oily.

From her messages, it seemed like Denis was the only guy Mom had been contacting often, but she'd mostly just given him her e-mail and arranged phone calls. She had messages from him as recent as a few days before she left. If she'd gone to visit a guy, this was probably the one.

I pulled up the WhitePages website, looking for a Denis Longwell in San Diego, California. The search brought up three listings for D. Longwells. I copied down the listings with a pencil from the reference desk. If I could get Dad to drive me out there, we could easily check that many. If he could get over this constitutional-rights issue, he might even be proud of me.

I headed to the pay phone to leave Jamie another message, but when I got there, I had a different idea. Dad was pissed over Ian, but if I could help him get Ian back, maybe he'd be in a good enough mood to help me find Mom. I dialed Dad's cell—the phone that was still in the truck.

I wondered if the car or the cell phone could be tracked. In movies these things always had microchips that let people find bad guys, but since people still stole cars and phones and stuff, that probably didn't work in real life.

I jumped when Ian picked up the phone. "Bounty man's office," he said.

Tingles zipped through my ear. I hadn't really expected him to answer. I mean, if I was running around with a stolen cell phone, I wouldn't take incoming calls.

"That you, bounty man?"

"No," I said. "It's me. Ricki."

"Hey," Ian said. "Wasn't expecting you to call."

"So, where are you?" I asked.

"Where's your dad? He's not using you to get to me, is he?"

"No," I said. "He went to get a rental. He doesn't know I'm calling."

"What'd you call me for, then?"

"Um, because you stole our trailer, with all my stuff in it."

"Nah. Do you know how obvious that would be? I left the trailer a couple of blocks from the hotel. Tell your dad to get a rental with a trailer hitch."

"What are you giving me advice for? You're the one who got us into this."

"Hey, you know I didn't mean for you to get caught

up in it. It's not your fault bounty man's dragging you along."

If Ian was being nice to me, maybe I should be nice to him back. If he trusted me, he might let me know where he'd gone. Dad could sure use a lead, as bad as this chase was going.

"I wish I'd been there when you grabbed the car," I said.

"So you could stop me?"

"So I could see you again."

Ian laughed. "I stole your ride, girl. Why would you want to see me?"

"Well, it's nice to see someone standing up to my dad."

"You should try it sometime. It's not that hard."

"I stand up to him," I said. "I just never thought to steal the truck. Where are you taking it, anyway?"

"Why do you want to know?" he asked. "You going to run and tell your dad?"

I needed him to trust me. "Are you kidding me? He yelled at me for not watching the truck. If I told him I talked to you, he'd lose it."

"Yeah, well, even so. Better if you don't have anything to hide, right?"

I exaggerated a sigh. "Fine. Don't tell me."

"Aw, come on. Don't be like that."

Now I needed to choose my words carefully, so that Ian would believe me. "I thought maybe I'd come meet you, after I get away from my dad. If I knew where you were going."

Ian paused for a second. "You'd want to do that?"

"Well, sure," I said.

"Why, exactly?"

I thought for a second. And then the answer came to me, almost too easily. "I think my mom ran off to San Diego. Since you need to keep moving, maybe you could help me find her?" I was pretty proud of myself for coming up with that so quickly.

"You want me to take you to California?"

"Sure. You game?"

"Yeah, okay," Ian said. "But how are you going to get to me?"

"I don't know. Hitchhike?"

"That's pretty dangerous for a cute girl like you."

My cheeks flushed a little. I was doing this to help Dad, wasn't I?

"Look, how about this," he said. "You tell your dad where I'm going, and he'll bring you to me. Then we'll take off. How's that sound?"

I paused. "You really want me to tell Dad where you're going? Why would you do that?"

"Do you know how fun your dad is to mess with?"

I almost laughed. "So where are you going?" I asked.

"I'm headed east. My sister lives in Des Moines, so I'll be at her place. I bet your dad can find it if you tell him that much. Make him do some work. Think it's his idea. That kind of thing."

"Okay," I said. "Then what?"

"Then you and me'll meet up. Head to San Diego or wherever."

My heart beat faster. This was all sounding too doable. I couldn't run off to San Diego with Ian, could I? That would be exactly the kind of ballsy thing Ian kept telling me to do.

But I wouldn't. I'd tell Dad it was a setup. That would be the smart thing.

"I'll see you in Des Moines," I said.

"See you there."

And then the dial tone buzzed in my ear.

I kept the phone pressed against my cheek for a second longer. Had Ian told me the truth? Maybe he wasn't even headed to Des Moines. If I was in his position, I'd have lied to keep my dad off my back.

Even still, I had to tell Dad about the conversation. That was the only way to be sure I didn't really intend to run off with Ian.

But as I sat on the curb to wait, the doubt kept poking

at me, like a kid who didn't want to hear no. I couldn't help wondering, if I did run off with Ian, how long would Dad keep tracking us? And if he found Ian first, which would be more important to him—finding me, or turning in his skip?

North Platte, Nebraska.

Days since Mom left: 31.

Distance from San Diego, California: 1336.63 miles.

 **12**

The sky was dark by the time Dad showed up. Yellow floodlights lit the parking lot, and patrons gave me worried looks as they left. I just sat there with my feet in the gutter.

Dad parked a little blue sedan along the curb. I could see the outline of Stan in the dim back seat.

I stood as Dad climbed out of the car. "Sorry it took so long," he said. "I got a lead on Ian. He tried to use that credit card on I-80 toward Lincoln. He's headed east. One of the addresses I have is for his sister out in Des Moines, so he might be going there."

"He is," I said.

Dad leaned against the car. "What makes you so sure?"

"I called him."

"You called him."

"Right. I called your cell phone."

"You forgot he stole it?"

"No. I was trying to help you out."

Dad lowered his chin, casting shadows across his face. "I said I'd give you more to do. But I didn't tell you to start projects of your own."

"It wasn't a project. I just called him."

"And he happened to tell you where he's headed."

I had to be careful. He'd be pissed if he knew I'd suggested I might run away with Ian. "I think he wants you to chase him," I said. "I think he's having fun."

Dad rolled his eyes. "Great," he said. "That's just great."

I hugged my arms around my waist, balancing on the edge of the curb. "I was trying to help. At least now you know where to find him."

"First we're taking Stan back to Denver," Dad said. "Then we'll deal with Ian."

That would mean we wouldn't be getting up to Des Moines for at least a day. How long would Ian wait for us? "Shouldn't we go after him now?"

"You quit worrying," Dad said. "We'll talk more after I drop off Stan."

I walked around to the passenger door and pulled it open. "The trailer's parked a couple of blocks from the hotel, just so you know."

Dad sighed, walking around to the driver's side. "I don't want to mess with it right now. I want to get this job done."

I climbed into the car. A pine air freshener hung from the rearview mirror, making the car smell like it'd been scrubbed in Pine-Sol. Whoever designed that scent had obviously never smelled a real pine tree.

"We should at least stop by the trailer," I said. "Grab some clothes and stuff." Suddenly I felt like the adult, making sure we had everything we needed.

Dad looked at me like he was surprised I'd actually had a good idea. "Yeah, okay," he said. "Wouldn't want it to get towed."

Stan leaned between our seats. I caught a whiff of him and was grateful for the pine freshener. "Find that boy of yours yet, Max?" he asked.

"We've got some leads. But don't worry. We'll take you to Denver first."

"You don't need to do that," Stan said. "I'm happy to ride along."

Dad shook his head. "It's getting late. Besides, I'm not taking any more chances. Better a bird in hand than two in the bush."

Stan laughed. "I suppose that makes me your turkey, huh, Max?"

"Sure are."

Stan made a series of gobbling noises and then fell back in his seat, cracking up.

Dad drove back by the Ramada and began circling the surrounding blocks, looking for the trailer.

"Did you check your phone records, too?" I asked. "He might call ahead to his sister."

"I'll do it in the morning."

"How's that going to help?" Stan asked.

Dad laughed. "Why? You taking notes?"

"What'd I want to do that for? Hiding's too much work for me. Besides, I never know when you're coming till you show up."

"Too true," Dad said.

The trailer was parked outside a drugstore, and the owners weren't excited about us leaving it in their parking lot. Dad had thought to get a rental with a trailer hitch, so we ended up towing the trailer to an RV park and leaving it there. I said we should take it with us, but Dad didn't want it getting stolen again. Considering Ian knew we were coming, that seemed like a pretty good call to me.

What with getting the trailer settled and our bags packed, we didn't reach Denver until after midnight. When we dropped Stan off at the jail, he turned around to grin at me and wave good-bye. I waved back. I wondered if he'd ever manage to get his life together. He seemed happy the way he was, but it was a tragic kind of happy—the kind that just wandered around, never arriving anywhere. I knew guys like that at school, who migrated about bumming cigarettes and breaking hearts and occasionally ambling into class. I'd thought that was something a person grew out of, but I guessed Stan hadn't.

When Dad got back to the car after dropping Stan off, he was scowling.

"Do you think he's going to be okay?" I asked.

"Define 'okay.'"

"Do you think you'll have to pick him up again?"

"Probably. They might throw him in jail for longer this time, though. He's racked up quite a record."

Would Stan keep smiling in prison? I could imagine him leaning through the bars, begging the guards to bring him a drink.

"Doesn't it ever make you sad?"

"What?"

"All these people and their messed-up lives."

"Sure," Dad said. "Stan especially. He's a pleasant enough guy. But he's also an alcoholic, and he lets his addiction run his life."

That was probably true. It seemed like he had a mom who cared about him, even if she did turn him in to the law.

"At least he doesn't have any kids," I said.

"He did," Dad said.

"What?"

"He had a daughter, but she died, and his wife left him. He'll get around to telling you the whole story if he sobers up enough. I've heard it twice."

"Is that why he drinks so much?"

"I think that's how it started. Now I think it's just an addiction, and it'll carry on until he gets some help."

"And that doesn't make you feel bad?"

Dad switched lanes, heading toward a motel. "Sure it makes me feel bad for him. But it doesn't change the job."

"Have you ever thought about helping people, instead of hauling them off to jail?"

Dad was quiet for a moment. "Stan's more likely to get the support he needs by facing the consequences than he is bumming around bars. It's a chance for him to realize he's doing wrong."

"Then why isn't he getting better?"

"Because he's choosing not to. He's been sentenced to court-mandated rehab before. But he's not ready to change, so he slips out the first chance he gets."

"Isn't there anything else you can do for him?"

"Look, prison isn't just about cells anymore. There are counselors and probation officers—lots of people to help the skips figure out what's wrong and fix it. But that's not my job. My part ends when I take them in."

"Maybe that's not enough. Maybe people need you to be more involved in their lives." I wasn't sure when I had switched from talking about skips to talking about me, but somewhere I had, and Dad hadn't followed.

"Nah. I'm pretty good at the part I do. As long as skips keep jumping bail, someone has to bring them in. Leave it to the pros to help them change."

I leaned my head back against my seat. We shouldn't have been having this conversation right now. I was way too tired to make any sense.

Dad got quiet then and let out a long, slow breath. He just sat there, staring straight ahead, putting on his blinker to pull in to the motel. Maybe I wasn't the only one who didn't know how to say what I needed to say.

I expected Dad to chew me out about calling Ian after we got to the motel, but he took off almost immediately to go to one of his mysterious meetings. If it wasn't a girlfriend, I just hoped it wasn't hookers. If it was, I really didn't want the details. Instead I turned on the TV and watched *America's Greatest Chef.*

I wished I had my notebook, but that was still in the truck. I snagged the notepad in the hotel, intending to write down the details of the motel room. Instead I started listing the things I remembered about our last apartment—the bar stools where Mom and I would sit to eat breakfast, the bathroom filled with Mom's hair stuff, my own room with my photo collages all over the walls. Mom on a park bench with her friend Rachel. Jamie on the back of his cousin's motorcycle, trying to look all tough. Me and Anna on the park swings in the middle of the night. Taking down the photos when we switched apartments was a pain, but I always put them right back up again. That's what made my room look like mine.

Now they were all in Grandma's basement in a box. In Dad's trailer I didn't have a wall.

Tears snuck into my eyes. I went into the bathroom and wiped them. Then I took a long, hot shower, enjoying being in a real bathtub rather than a plastic stall where I couldn't shave my legs without my butt hitting the wall.

When I came out, Dad was back, and he'd flipped the channel to some crime drama. I closed my eyes and thought about Ian grinning at me from the back seat. I was pretty sure he was better looking in my memory than he was in real life, but I smiled and snuggled down in the clean sheets, glad to have a real bed to sleep in.

Dad woke me by calling my name. I glanced up at the clock, 5:00 a.m. I'd had less than four hours' sleep.

"Get up," he said. "Time to go find our boy."

It took us about ten minutes to get on the road, since

we had next to nothing to pack. I slept an extra two hours in the car. When I woke again, the sky was finally starting to get light.

"I guess you can't do homework," Dad said. "Since Ian took it with him. Maybe you'll get lucky and he'll complete your assignments for you."

"Not likely."

"No kidding. Look, we need to talk anyway."

When Mom said that, she'd have meant that she wanted advice about a relationship, or that she wanted details about mine. She'd come into my room and sit on the end of my bed, flopping back and hugging a pillow. "Ricki," she'd say, "we need to talk."

"About what?" I said, even though I already knew.

"About you calling Ian."

"I told you before, I was trying to help you out."

Dad sighed and took a long time to respond, like he was trying to figure out what to do with me. "I said I'd give you more to do if you proved you could do what I say. But you haven't managed to do that even once."

"It's not my fault things keep going wrong. In case you haven't noticed, your job isn't exactly predictable."

Dad sighed. "That's exactly why I didn't want you involved in the first place."

This wasn't going in a good direction. I softened my tone.

"I know the job with Ian is going badly. But it's not fair for you to blame it on me. I watched Stan yesterday, just like you asked. I kept track of him, even though it was hard 'cause he went into the bar. I know you were pissed that I left the truck, so I thought I could make it up to you by finding out where Ian was. That's all."

That was mostly all, anyway. I didn't hate the idea of seeing Ian again, but Dad didn't need to hear about that.

Dad's eyes flicked to me for a second and then back to the road. He clicked on his blinker, merging onto the freeway.

"I'm sorry," he said. "You're right. I knew this job was too chaotic for a fifteen-year-old. I don't know what got into my head, letting you help like that."

He wished I wasn't here. That wasn't what he was supposed to say. "Let me have another chance," I said.

Dad's lips pressed together. "I can't put you in danger like that again."

"I was talking on a phone. That's not dangerous."

"Depends who's on the other end. Ian isn't just a guy. We talked about this. He's a criminal."

"So he made some mistakes. That doesn't make him different from us."

"He broke the law. That's the difference."

"So because ignoring your daughter for fifteen years

151

isn't against the law, that makes it okay." This had to be the lack of sleep talking. I never would have said that if I was in my right mind.

Dad's hands tightened on the wheel, and I scooted closer to the door. "I'm sorry I haven't been a great father. But I didn't ignore you. I sent cards. Paid child support. I picked you up from Grandma's. I always fulfilled my legal obligations to your mother. You ask her."

"You saw me at Grandma's a couple of times *in my life*. You even forgot my birthday half the time."

"I always remembered your birthday. I just didn't always call. Look, I'd fix it if I could, but I can't redo any of it."

That made me want to punch him in the face. "I think I know where Mom might be," I said.

Dad's face shifted, but I couldn't quite tell what he was feeling. I couldn't read him the way I could read Mom.

"How's that?" Dad asked.

"I got into her e-mail. But I need you to help me finish tracking her down."

Dad shook his head.

"I need her back, you know."

"She left you," Dad said. "I never thought she'd do that. Thought she'd be a better mother to you than she was a wife to me. So I paid your support and stayed out of her way."

I rested my arm on the cracked leather armrest, tapping my index finger over and over. I wanted to defend Mom, tell him she was a good mother. But she wasn't here now.

"It would have been easier to come live with you if I'd seen you more often," I said. "Wouldn't have killed you to drop by."

"Wasn't that I didn't want to see you," Dad said. "I kept your picture right here." He pulled his wallet out of his back pocket, revealing an old, yellowed picture of me—my second-grade school photo. One of my front teeth was missing, and you could see my tongue poking through the hole.

"I'm seven in that picture," I said. "That's not me."

"It's still you," Dad said. "That's the way I remember you."

"Well, I'm different now. If you'd been around, you would have noticed."

Dad sighed. "I'm sorry, Ricki. I've been trying, over the last year. I know it seems way too late, but I'm trying."

"What changed?" I asked. "Why suddenly start calling when I'm fifteen years old?"

Dad was silent for a long moment, but something in his face told me not to interrupt this silence. I held my breath, waiting. I needed an answer. Any answer, except that he didn't want me.

"I got sober," Dad said finally. "That's what changed."

That stopped me. "You what?"

Dad reached into the ashtray of his truck and pulled out a large coin. He flipped it at me, and I caught it.

"That's my eighteen-month chip," Dad said. "It means I haven't had a drink in a year and a half."

"And before that?"

"Before that, I drank."

I stared down at the coin. It had a triangle on it, and the words "Unity," "Service," and "Recovery" that explained his mysterious meetings.

"I didn't know that."

"Now you do."

"Were you like Stan?"

"I kept it together a lot better than him. I held this job, most of the time. I supported myself, and I steered clear of the law. But I also did a lot of things I regret."

"Like what?"

"Like ignored my daughter, for one."

I turned the coin over in my hand. Dad started calling me a year ago. That'd be six months after he got sober.

"I wish I could change all that," Dad said. "But I can't."

"Would you?" I asked. "If you could do it over again?"

Dad shook his head. "If I could do it over again," he said, "I'd skip that party where I met your mom."

I stared out at the road, watching the yellow dashes slide past the windshield wipers one after another.

He wished that I didn't exist. Then he wouldn't have to feel guilty that he hadn't been around. That probably would have been better for Mom, too. Then she wouldn't have to worry about me when she headed off to have fun.

"Sure," I said, trying to ignore my tingling tear ducts. "That probably would have been easier on everyone."

Dad looked at me, shaking his head. "Nah, Ricki," he said. "I didn't mean it like that. I meant you should have had another father. One who wasn't too drunk to be around. One who could have given your mother what she needed."

What did Mom need? Mom always told me she didn't need a man for good, just to play with now and then, and brush off when she got bored. But what kind of husband had Dad been? Had he hurt her so bad with his drinking that she'd given up on men? I tried to picture what Dad would be like drunk, but I couldn't. And I didn't have enough memories of him to remember ever seeing him drink.

"I still don't see why you couldn't have been around more. Even if you were drinking."

Dad sighed. "Seeing her brought back too many memories. Made a mess of me, made me want the liquor even more. I couldn't take you out and stay sober, and I knew you deserved a better father than that. I just didn't believe I had it in me."

Mom and Dad had separated before Mom even knew she was pregnant, and divorced by my first birthday. Surely he could have gotten over it sometime in the last fifteen years. But I thought about Stan, drinking because of his dead kid and his lost wife—because he had an addiction and couldn't stop.

"And now?" I asked.

Dad stayed quiet, and I thought he was going to cop out of the conversation again.

"Well?" I said.

"Now I think that was bullshit," Dad said. "I think I could have changed all along, I was just too damn scared."

"You're right," I said. "I did deserve better."

Dad nodded, eyes glued to the road.

I hated it when people did that—just let you insult them without arguing back. It made me feel guilty, which I probably deserved. A good daughter would have said she was proud of the way he finally decided to change. A good daughter would have been able to forgive him, now that she knew the truth. But I couldn't help feeling like I'd finally learned for certain the thing I'd been so afraid of all these years: he loved his other life more than me. The fact that the other life was alcohol rather than being a superhero didn't soften the blow.

Tears burned into my eyes. I leaned toward the window, resting my temple against the glass. If Ian wasn't full of shit, he'd be waiting for me in Des Moines, thinking I was planning to slip away from Dad and take off to California with him. To find Mom. There were only three D. Longwells in San Diego. If I couldn't find Denis, I'd send Mom a letter at our old address. And Ian would be with me every step of the way—helping me out in ways that Dad flatly refused to.

But here Dad was, finally telling me the truth. That had to count for something. Still, it had taken him six months to contact me once he was sober, and he hadn't come to get me until Grandma insisted. He had no other choice. He was stuck with me.

I held my breath, blinking back the tears and watching the yellow line continuing to whiz by. We'd be in Des Moines in a few hours. If Dad cared, he'd follow after me, wouldn't he? And if he didn't, well, he could just go back to his regular life, and I could find Mom and get back to mine.

That was a crazy idea, and I knew it. I wanted to be near Ian, but he was also on the run from the law, and if I went with him, I would be too. But if I stayed with

Dad, I'd never know if he really wanted me now or if he was just taking care of me because he had to. I closed my eyes to keep the tears from welling out. They pooled in the corners, and I brushed at them with one hand, wiping them away before Dad noticed.

I couldn't know what I should do until I saw whether or not Ian was really waiting for me. I'd just have to figure it out when we got to Des Moines.

Des Moines, Iowa.
Days since Mom left: 32.
Distance from San Diego, California: 1749.41 miles.

13

We reached Des Moines around one o'clock. Flat, gray clouds stretched across the sky, and fat rain-drops pelted the windshield, running in ripples as the wind blew them toward the edges. Dad had been quiet for most of the ride, which was just as well, because I didn't want to talk to him, either. Dad used an actual map to get to Ian's sister's house, since his GPS was still in the truck. As we pulled down her street, I caught sight of our red pickup parked crookedly against the curb.

Dad grinned. "We got him," he said.

My spine prickled. Had Ian actually stuck around? Did that mean he was hiding somewhere, waiting for me?

"I need you out of the way," Dad said, "but I know you're not going to stay in the car."

My skin tingled. If I got out of the car, I might really run off with Ian. And then what? "I will this time," I said. "I promise."

Dad chewed on his cheek. I could tell he was wrestling with wanting to trust me and knowing he couldn't.

He was right.

I held up my palm. "I will stay in the car. I swear." Even I was afraid of what I might do if I didn't.

"All right," Dad said, but I wasn't sure if it was because he was giving me another chance or because he didn't have another good option.

Dad parked two houses away from the truck and got out, taking the keys with him. He trusted me, but not that much.

My heart picked up pace. If Ian really was waiting for me, he'd wait for Dad to go inside and then come get me. But I'd told Dad I'd stay in the car, so I would. That was the smarter thing to do, right?

I didn't watch as Dad walked up to the house. Ian probably wasn't here. If he was smart, he'd already run off in some other stolen car and left Dad's truck behind for us to find. He'd probably just told me he'd wait for me to lead us in the wrong direction.

I leaned back in my seat and closed my eyes. I took long breaths, trying to calm down.

The car still smelled of Stan's body odor and a faint tinge of beer. I opened my eyes, looking up at the sky. The raindrops thinned a bit, and I cracked my window. Better wet than stinky, anyway.

I jumped when I saw Ian's face grinning at me through the driver's-side window. I looked back at the house, but Dad was nowhere in sight. Ian reached for the door handle. Dad hadn't locked his door, probably so he could run back to the car in a hurry if he needed.

Ian opened the door and rested a hand on it. He bent over, leaning into the car.

"Hey," he said. "You ready for a ride?"

Stay in the car, I told myself. You promised. "You really waited for me?"

"I said I would, didn't I?" Ian sat down in the driver's seat. I expected him to beckon me out of the car, but instead he pulled out a key ring full of thin, key-shaped strips of metal. They looked like some kind of child's toy— too thin to be real keys.

Ian shoved one in the ignition and shook it up and down.

"What is that?" I asked.

"Auto jigglers," he said. "Give me a second."

I looked back toward the house. The door was open, but Dad had disappeared inside.

This couldn't be happening. I sat totally still in my seat. I'd sworn to Dad I would stay in the car. I just hadn't expected Ian to steal it with me inside.

Ian pulled the first jiggler out of the lock and inserted another one.

"Where did you get those things?" I asked.

Ian grinned. "Why, you looking to get into the business?" He pulled the second key out and moved on to a third. As he shook it, the ignition popped, and the engine turned over.

"Nice," Ian said. He revved the engine and threw the car in gear.

This was happening. This was real. I glanced back at the house in time to see Dad running down the front steps.

Ian didn't wait for me to say anything. He just slammed the door. Hearing the noise, Dad looked up, and his jaw actually dropped. Ian gave him a little wave and then gunned it down the street at top speed.

I watched out the window as Dad raced for the truck, and then Ian skidded around a corner, headed for the highway.

"This is no good," I said. "He's totally going to catch us."

Ian grinned, running a hand through his hair. "He'll have to find his brake pads first."

"His *brake pads?*" I leaned forward in my seat, clasping my knees. "Aren't those important?"

"Chill out."

"No, seriously. He could get in an accident."

Ian shook his head. "Nah. The car will still *stop*. It'll just eat into the rotors on the way. Might take him a while to fix."

That didn't sound nearly as bad, but I still worried. I'd done exactly what Dad asked me to, but everything still went wrong—like when I'd followed Stan into the bar.

But this was what I wanted, wasn't it? Now I'd get to see if Dad would really follow—if he'd really worry about me when I wasn't right there with him.

"You okay?" Ian asked.

"What?"

"You just seem unsure. You're not having second thoughts, are you?"

"No," I said, even though I was. My nails ran in grooves over the armrest. What if Dad didn't find us? Could I really track Mom down in San Diego? Suddenly I wasn't so sure.

"I guess you can add vandalism to your list of crimes," I said, trying to sound casual.

Ian just laughed. He was driving so fast toward the freeway exit that I was sure a cop would pull us over, but apparently there weren't any nearby. We broke out onto the freeway, doing eighty up the on-ramp.

"Maybe you should slow down," I said.

"Hey, what's the problem?" Ian asked. "This was your idea, wasn't it?" He gave me a sidelong glance.

The speedometer needle descended down the right side of the dial.

"You know, my dad says this is how stolen cars get found."

"Huh?"

"Speeding. Dad says cops don't spend a lot of time looking for stolen cars, so usually they get found when the driver breaks the law."

Ian looked at the speed gauge and slowed down about ten miles per hour. "Good tip," he said. "You're a smart girl. We make a good team."

"Sure," I said.

Ian glanced over at my arm, which was still fidgeting with the armrest. "You sure you're okay?"

"Yeah, I'm sure," I said quickly. Too quickly.

His lips tightened into a line. "No, you're not. It's cool if you've changed your mind. You want me to drop you somewhere?"

My heart thudded. "You'd do that?"

"Sure. What? Did you think I was going to hold you for ransom or something?"

"Of course not."

"Look, if you want, I can drop you off and you can call your dad. The cell phone's in the truck."

I leaned back in my seat, trying to relax. I wasn't stuck here. I could stop and call Dad at any time. I still had his business card in my wallet, but I also had the addresses of those D. Longwells in San Diego. I had choices.

And if we stopped now, I'd never know how far Dad would follow me.

"No," I said. "Keep driving."

"All right," Ian said. "Where to?"

"You're still going to help me find my mom, right?"

"Sure, if you still want to find her. I'd say good riddance, if I were you."

"Quit talking me out of it."

"I just want you to be sure. San Diego's a big city, you know."

"I know the name of the guy she's with. I've got some addresses we can try."

"That's a start."

That's when I thought past the driving part. What if Dad didn't catch us right away? He'd fall behind if he couldn't drive the truck. Where were we going to stay on the way? Could we drive straight through to California? What if Mom hadn't gone to see Denis at all? Was I going to end up living with Ian—like, in an apartment—or sleeping with him in the car?

"Um, do you know anyone in San Diego we can stay with?" I asked. "In case it takes a while to find her?"

Ian laughed. "We'll meet some people. Don't worry."

But I did worry. I'd made a promise to Dad that I'd stay in the car, which I'd done. But we both knew that promise was a promise to stay out of trouble, which was the opposite of what I'd done. Even if Dad did chase me, he might never trust me again. I could end up in foster care. Or juvie. I could end up a skip like Ian.

"Why are you running away, anyway?" I asked. "Don't all the charges you're racking up amount to more than you'd get just turning yourself in? The sentence for stealing one car can't be that bad."

"Twenty-nine."

"What?"

"Twenty-nine cars."

I gaped at him. "Why would you steal twenty-nine cars?"

"You know how much a car is worth?"

"Depends on the car," I said. "So you were selling them?"

"Didn't say I was selling them. I was *charged* with selling them. The cops thought there was this whole crime-ring thing."

"Well, was there?" I looked out the window at the blur of wet concrete, trying to loosen the knots in my shoulders.

Ian stepped on the gas again. "Screw it," he said. "If we go that slow, bounty man'll catch us."

"Hey, maybe we should get off the road for a while," I said. The car was speeding us toward California every minute, and if we pulled over for a while, I'd have time to think. If I wanted Dad to find me, I needed to give him the chance.

"You sure? We should probably put more distance between us and the man."

"Dad says people who make beelines down main highways are supereasy to catch." Dad never said any such thing, but it seemed like it might be true. "It'd be harder to find us if we pulled off on one of these farm roads for a while and then drove when he doesn't expect us to be here."

"All right." Ian watched for the next side off-ramp and then pulled down a side road. He drove alongside a field, then parked and climbed out of the car. I followed. The sky was still cloudy, but the rain had stopped for the moment, leaving the ground damp. I took a deep breath, taking in the smell of fresh rain and wet dirt, following Ian along the fence that bordered the field.

"Do you think you can see the car from the road?" he asked.

I couldn't tell, and I didn't want to walk back to the road to check. "We're probably safe," I said.

Ian hopped up onto the fence and swung his legs over, facing the field.

"So what's your mom doing in San Diego?" he asked.

"I think she's staying with some guy she met online."

"So she left you with your dad to chase after this guy?"

"No," I said. "She left me with my grandma, but Grandma called Dad."

"Shouldn't you be in school or something?"

"Shouldn't you?"

"Nah," Ian said. "They weren't teaching me anything important anyway."

"Yeah. I guess schools don't teach you how to steal cars."

"It's not like I was planning to do that forever, you know."

"So you admit to it, then."

Ian just smiled, looking out at the field. Whatever grew here had already been harvested; all that was left was a piece of rusted watering equipment and row after row of broken soil.

Now that we weren't in a car, moving ever farther away from Dad, I started to relax.

"What are you going to do next?" I asked.

"I don't know. Whatever comes along. That's the

beauty of this life. You take the chances that come to you. Maybe I'll buy a car dealership." He waved at the field. "Maybe I'll be a farmer."

I sincerely doubted Ian had the money to buy a dealership. "You want to be a farmer?"

"Maybe I do and I just don't know it yet."

I looked over the field. This was somebody's life, I guess. "What do you think they were growing?" I asked.

"Maybe weed."

I laughed. "In a field like this? They'd get caught."

"You're right. Probably something boring like radishes, then."

"You'd grow weed, in your field."

"Maybe not in a field. Maybe in a closet. I could look into grow lights." He raised his eyebrows at me, and I tried to decide if he was joking.

Sitting this close, I could see little flecks of green in his eyes, spread outward in tiny spirals. "Thanks for offering to help me find my mom. That's more than my dad would do."

"Yeah, well, you can't sit around waiting for them to get it together. You've got to take charge of your life."

I'd taken charge all right. Taken charge right into the middle of Nowhere, Iowa. "I think I'm bad at it," I said.

Ian laughed. "Yeah, well, no one's perfect. Keep trying. You'll get it right."

That was ironic, coming from a fugitive. "Have you gotten it right yet?"

"Hell no. But I will. And so will you."

I still wasn't convinced that was true, but it was nice of him to say it. "Thanks," I said.

"No problem." Ian ducked his head a little, bringing it closer to mine. "So, are we still going to San Diego, or should I drop you somewhere else?"

"Do you really want to go with me to California?"

Ian shrugged. "California's probably the same as every damn place."

"Yeah. Probably."

Ian lifted his arm, and I slipped under it, letting him rest it on my shoulders. His spicy smell mixed with the scent of dirt and rain, until the breeze picked up and blew it away.

Ian inclined his face toward mine, and I raised my chin slightly, until his nose brushed up against mine. Just a few more inches. Just a bend of his neck. Just a lift of my chin.

Ian's head snapped up as an unfamiliar car turned down the piece of road behind our rental, tires crunching in the gravel. The car didn't even stop fully before Dad jumped out and stood there, gun pointed straight at Ian. Straight at me.

Outside Des Moines, Iowa.
Days since Mom left: 32.
Distance from Salt Lake City, Utah: 1053.5 miles.

14

I froze, staring at Dad's gun. His face was expressionless.

"Step away from her," Dad said. "Ricki, get in the car."

A cold wave washed through me. He *was* worried about me.

"I mean it, Ricki. Get in the car *now*."

I looked at the unfamiliar car and then at the rental. "Which one?" I asked.

"The Camry." He glared at Ian. "Step away from her, hands in the air."

Ian's face hardened, but he raised his arm from my shoulder and kicked off the fence and into the field, his feet sinking a little in the dirt. It wasn't until then that I realized he'd left his arm there when he saw Dad—hadn't pulled it away or anything. Like he was daring Dad to do something about it.

I scrambled off the fence in the other direction and stepped over to the unfamiliar car, double checking to make sure it actually was the Camry.

"Drop the keys," Dad said to Ian.

Ian spit in Dad's direction.

"Hands behind your head," Dad barked. He popped the trunk of the rental and pulled out a pair of cuffs, sticking them on Ian and hauling him over to the car. He glared at me through the window, and I looked away, staring at the dash.

After Dad had secured Ian in the back seat, he climbed in on the driver's side, not even looking at me.

"I'm so sorry, Dad," I said.

"Not now," he said back.

I chewed the inside of my cheek. His tone was so clipped, he might be pissed enough to put me in foster care. A lot of good it did to know he'd chase me, if running this time was the final blow that made him give up on me.

"I did stay in the car," I said. "Like I promised."

"Yeah, you did exactly what you said. Very clever."

I felt like sinking right through the seat. He knew we'd planned this. The promise I made hadn't been part of the plan, but I couldn't convince Dad of that. "But—"

"Ricki, shut up," Dad said. "We'll talk about it later."

We settled into silence. Raindrops slapped against the windshield again, and Dad stepped on the accelerator, driving the Camry back to Des Moines.

It turned out the Camry belonged to Ian's sister. Dad had borrowed her car after he busted his brakes.

After we got back to Ian's sister's place, she came with us to pick up the rental, since we had to leave it by the field. Dad offered to let her drive her own car, but instead she climbed into the back seat, plunking herself down next to Ian.

"You said you were trying to get away from some people," she said. "You never told me you were running from the law."

Ian shrugged. "You didn't ask."

"I shouldn't *have* to ask." She leaned toward Dad. "What'd he do, anyway?"

"Credit card fraud," Dad said. "Vandalism. Kidnapping."

"I haven't been charged with any of that."

"But you will be," Dad said.

I heard a slap and twisted around to see the sister's arm coming down after smacking Ian in the back of the head.

"Hey, now," Dad said. "Let's all calm down."

The sister shook her head. "This is so stupid. You know better."

"Right, because our family is full of so many fine examples."

"How long are you going to use Dad as an excuse for your stupidity?"

Ian didn't respond; he just stared at the window, face hard. I wished for my notebook to record that look.

When we got to the field, Dad transferred Ian to the rental car. Dad pulled the set of jigglers out of the ignition and locked them in the trunk, and the sister got in the driver's seat of her car and drove off without even saying good-bye. When we went back to her house for the truck, she hadn't returned.

Dad hitched the truck up to the rental car.

"We'll tow it back to North Platte," he said. "We can at least stay in the trailer while we wait for it to be fixed. He also grabbed his chains out of the truck and bound Ian's feet together. He'd cuffed Ian's hands behind his back this time. Ian looked pretty uncomfortable, arms stuck behind him so he couldn't lean back without his shoulders bowing out unnaturally.

Ian started to say something as we drove back down I-80, but Dad snapped at him before he got a breath out.

"Whatever it is, I don't want to hear it," Dad said.

"Hey," Ian said, "if you're so set on taking me to jail,

why don't you just drop me off at the station and be done with it?"

Dad couldn't do that. We had to get back to the jail in the county of the arrest, or Dad wouldn't get paid. This trip had already been expensive, especially now that Dad had to fix his brakes.

Dad didn't explain that to Ian, though. He just said, "I told you to shut up."

By the time we got to North Platte the sun had set. Most places had closed, but Dad found a mechanic attached to a gas station who agreed to look at the truck. Dad double checked that Ian was chained securely in the back of the car, then parked it right next to the window of the auto mechanic so he could keep an eye on him while he was making arrangements to get the truck fixed.

"You're coming in too," Dad said to me. "No arguments."

I didn't argue, just followed him into the shop. The mechanic spotted us through an open door to the back and shouted, "Be there in a few." I looked around. There was only one guy working.

Dad took a seat next to the window, where he could see Ian clearly. Ian leaned back in his seat, his eyes closed, but Dad still stared at him.

The silence was killing me. When Mom was pissed at

me, she'd march into the room yelling straight off. But Dad just sat there, stewing and avoiding. I hated knowing the fight was coming; I wanted to get it over with.

"Can we talk now?" I asked. It came out sounding snotty when I hadn't meant it to.

Dad shook his head at me, his voice quiet and low. "Did you have something to say for yourself?"

"How'd you find us?"

"I could see the car from the freeway."

"But how did you know which way we'd gone?"

"You had to have gone one way or the other. I guessed. Do you have any idea how dangerous that was?"

"I am really, really sorry."

"I should never have put you in this situation to begin with. Ian is a manipulator—maybe a better one than either of us. You shouldn't be near him."

I wanted to explain to Dad what I'd been doing with Ian—to come up with some way to tell Dad that I'd wanted him to save me. But I didn't know how to say that in any way that sounded sane. Maybe because it wasn't. "I know," I said at last. "I'm sorry."

"We'll get Ian back to Denver as soon as the truck is fixed. Then this'll all be over with."

"And then what?" I asked, setting myself down in an uncomfortable plastic chair. I couldn't bring myself to ask the real question: Are you going to give up on me now?

"We'll figure something out."

That wasn't a promise either way.

"If you found Mom, you wouldn't have to worry about me anymore," I said quietly. "You could just go back to your normal life."

Dad sighed. "I don't want to go over that again right now."

"Something must have happened to her. We should call the police."

"Your grandma already did, the first week she was gone. They took a report, since she abandoned a child. That's about all they'll do, though, unless they suspect foul play."

"She didn't abandon me," I said. Except that she had. I'd always thought of Dad as the abandoner, but that's what it's called when your parent leaves you and doesn't call.

My arms shook, so I crossed them securely in front of me.

Dad stared at the magazines on the counter. "It's not your fault. She did this to me, too."

I pushed up against the cold concrete wall of the corner, trying to get as far away from Dad as possible. "What do you mean?"

Dad's eyes flicked toward Ian again, and he sighed. "She walked out on me. I came home from work one day and she wasn't there. Left me a note saying she'd gone off with a girlfriend for a couple of days to Reno, but she'd packed most of her stuff with her. I waited for her to come back. Waited two months before I heard from her. And then she was just arranging to come back and pick up the rest of her crap. Said she'd filed for divorce. Never did tell me why. I didn't find out she was pregnant until six months later, when she called me from the hospital to tell me you'd been born."

I looked toward the empty register. I'd always thought Dad had left Mom. I knew Dad wasn't there when I was born, but I'd assumed he chose not to come.

What had Mom told me, exactly? I couldn't remember the words now.

"Was it because you were a drunk?" I asked.

"No. I didn't start drinking until after."

I wanted to snap at him that he was lying, that Mom would never walk out with no reason, but I bit my lip. She hadn't had a reason to walk out on me.

"So we're the same, you and me," Dad said. "Both of us cast off by the same woman."

I rested my head on my hands. Dad left me when I was a baby. Mom left me now. Jamie wouldn't e-mail me. Was there no one in my life who I could count on to stay?

"We're not the same," I said. "You're an adult. You could have been a part of our lives—that was your right as my father. But you weren't. Lots of people drink. It's not an excuse for abandoning me."

"You're right," Dad said. "It's not an excuse at all, but that doesn't change that it's the truth."

The mechanic stepped in from the shop, smiling at us. "What can I do you for?" he asked.

Dad and I both looked up at him, and his eyes flicked from Dad to me and back to Dad, his smile fading slightly. He tried again. "Something I can help you with?"

"Yeah," Dad said, standing. "Got a truck that needs new brakes." And just like that, he was back to business, leaving his daughter behind.

North Platte, Nebraska.
Days since Mom left: 32.
Distance from Salt Lake City, Utah: 1057.5 miles.

 # 15

I t turned out the truck couldn't be fixed until morning, since the mechanic had to wait for a part.

"We'll drive Ian back to Denver tonight in the rental," Dad said as we walked to the car.

We were about three yards from the car when I saw Ian's knees rise between the two front seats. He braced himself on the back seat with his cuffed hands, thrusting up with his pelvis and kicking his feet in the air, boots connecting with the windshield. Ian's chains slapped against the glass and it gave, showering over the dash in puzzlelike pieces.

Dad swore loudly, and the mechanic came running out to the parking lot, adding some choice words of his own.

"Fuck you, bounty man," Ian shouted through the hole in the windshield.

Dad just stared at him while the mechanic whistled at the damage.

"I'm going to need the truck towed to the RV park," Dad said, his voice eerily even. "And then back again in the morning."

"Are you sure you don't want to leave it all here?"

"No," Dad said. "I'm going to need someplace to put him."

The mechanic looked a little confused, but he didn't ask questions. "You want me to order a windshield while I'm at it?"

Dad sighed, then nodded. I wondered if rental places wanted you to do that or if they'd rather repair the damage themselves.

Ian just smiled.

Turned out the mechanic also had a tow truck, so he took the truck to the RV park himself. I shook my head as he backed the truck against our trailer. Here we were with three vehicles and nothing to drive.

Dad pushed Ian into the back seat of the broken-down truck and chained him to the floor, then motioned for me to follow as he stormed back toward the trailer. Dad got quieter as he got madder.

"What are we going to do?" I asked.

"We'll head out tomorrow," he said.

"Not until then?"

"That's right." His voice was so clipped, I knew I was pushing it.

"Why?"

"Part for the truck won't be in until then."

"Couldn't you get another rental car?"

Dad looked up at the sky. The clouds gathered darkly above us. "I'm too angry to drive," he said. "And I'm running on four hours of sleep. It's a long way back to Denver. Wouldn't be safe, with the storm coming."

"Okay." I didn't know what else to say. What I really needed was to connect with my old life—with my old self. I needed to call Anna.

Dad climbed into the trailer and left the door standing open for me.

"Can I use the phone?" I asked.

"No."

"But I need it."

"To call your grandmother?"

"No. A friend."

"What friend?"

"My friend Anna, from school."

"What do you need to call her for?"

"I just want to feel normal again."

Dad sighed. "Here." He handed me the phone. "Don't talk all night."

I took it. Dad kept the trailer door open, but instead of going in I walked past the RV office to the lamplit picnic area and parked my butt on one of the tables with my feet on the bench. I dialed Anna's number. A cold wind bit at me, and I cradled the phone in my hand to keep the air from blowing at the microphone.

The phone rang only once before she picked up. Like she'd been waiting for me to call.

"Ricki!" Anna said. "I was just going to call you."

"Really?" I asked.

"Yes. Are you doing okay? Have you heard from your mom?"

"Still no," I said. "I think she's in San Diego, but I'm not sure."

"When are you coming back? Can you stay with your grandma again?"

"I don't know." I'd have loved to get back home, though, with or without Mom. "Did your mom decide yet if I can stay with you?"

"She keeps insisting you're better off with family. I keep telling her we *are* family, but it's not working."

"Thanks for trying. Maybe I can hide in Jamie's basement or something." We both knew that was impossible: Jamie lived in a two-bedroom apartment.

"Look, I have to tell you something you don't want to hear."

I sucked in a breath. Maybe calling Anna had been a mistake.

"Remember how you told me to find out if Jamie was seeing someone else?"

There was only one way the conversation could go after that. This couldn't be happening. Not right now.

"Ricki, you still there? Can you hear me?"

It's not like I thought I'd be with Jamie forever. But he couldn't disappear on me without so much as an e-mail. He couldn't slip out of my life without giving me a reason, without giving me a choice. Just like Dad had. Just like Mom.

"I hear you," I said. "He's seeing someone else."

"I am so sorry, sweetie. He's a complete shitface."

"How can that be? I talked to him a week ago."

"From what I hear, he was already two-timing you then."

My brain melted into soup, and I held perfectly still so it wouldn't roll out my ears into a puddle. At least Mom had left me a note. Now Anna was the last real piece of my old life left. How long until she left me too? Would she even call when she did? Would she give me a reason?

"I've been telling everyone that he gave you crabs. It's more plausible than gonorrhea."

"So now everyone thinks I have crabs?"

"They'll have forgotten by the time you get back."

My body felt so limp, I thought I might fall off the table. Chances were, they'd have forgotten me entirely by then. "I've got to go," I said.

"You're not mad at me, are you?"

"No."

"He's an asshole. Seriously. You can do so much better."

"Thanks," I said. My voice came out flat and quiet.

"Call me when you're ready to talk. Anytime. Day or night. I'm sending you mental ice cream right now."

Triple Chocolate Devastation ice cream. That was the tradition. Anna and I would wait for Mom to get home so we could choc out together. We'd started doing that when I was twelve and broke up with my first real boyfriend, and Mom hadn't missed a breakup since.

But where the hell was Mom now? Where was she when I needed her?

I hung up the phone, wondering if I should e-mail Jamie and chew him out. I hadn't even asked Anna who he was screwing around with. I wasn't sure that I cared.

As I walked back to the trailer under the dim lamplight, my guts ached from the inside out. Wasn't I worth sticking around for? I couldn't even stay with Anna, since her mom didn't think I was family enough for them. Soon Anna would forget about me too. What was wrong with me that this kept happening?

I jerked open the trailer doors, stepping in. Dad sat at the table, peeling an orange. He looked up at me.

"Did you get your homework from the truck?" he asked.

"No," I said. My voice came out harsh and hysterical, and I wished I could snap the word back.

"Why not?"

"What do you care?" I crossed my arms over my chest. I knew I was being unreasonable, but I couldn't help it.

"I'm your father. That's why I care."

"Mom never bothered me about homework."

"Well, I'm not your mother."

"No shit," I said.

Dad looked up at me, his voice sharpening. "Watch your mouth."

I sounded like a child, and I knew it, but yelling at Dad turned my ache into a numbness. Raising my voice pushed back the pain.

"You get your work done, and I won't have to bother you about it," Dad said.

Neither of us cared about the homework. He was still pissed about me running away with Ian, and I was pissed about Jamie and Mom and everything else. For once, I wished we could have a fight about the real stuff.

"It doesn't matter," I said. "Give it a week and I'll be back with Mom and you'll be out of my life again."

Dad gave me a confused look, like he'd missed a turn. I took a step back, toward the bathroom. I shouldn't have said that. Fighting about homework was safer.

"I'm not going anywhere," Dad said.

"Well I am. Mom's coming back, and then I won't have to live here anymore."

I gestured around at the decrepit trailer, making sure he got the picture. Even as I said it, I knew I was wrong. Something had happened to her. She was probably lying in a ditch somewhere. She would *never* leave me for this long otherwise. If cops couldn't find stolen cars, it wasn't a surprise that they hadn't found her.

Dad stood up, facing me. I flattened myself against the bathroom door, hand on the knob. "I'm sorry your mom walked out on you," he said, "but you need to start facing the truth. Things aren't going back to the way they were. They can't."

Panic fluttered behind my ribs. He was right, of course. Nothing would ever be the same again, no matter how much I wanted it to be.

"She could be dead," I said. "And you won't even look for her."

"She's not dead," Dad said. "Leaving was her choice. You better figure that out fast, or you'll waste years of your life being bitter."

"Like you?"

"Yes, like me."

I hadn't really expected Dad to agree with me, so I didn't know where to go from there.

Dad leaned back against the fridge. "Look around, Ricki," he said. "I'm the one giving you a place to stay, even if you hate it. I'm sorry I can't provide more, I truly am, but who else in your life is trying to give you anything at all?"

Tears swelled up in my eyes, and I tried to blink them back, but the traitors ran right down my face.

Dad's face softened when he saw me start to cry, and the pain inside jabbed sharp and new. I couldn't take the sympathy, so I jerked open the bathroom door and squished myself inside, slamming it shut. "Leave me alone," I yelled through the pressboard door.

I heard Dad shift back to the table, heard the squish of the seat as he sat down, but he didn't say anything back.

I sat down on the toilet, kicking the thin wall separating me from the closet. The wall gave a little and I stopped. Ian had the guts to stick his foot through a windshield, but I didn't. I just went along with whatever they wanted—Mom, Dad, Jamie. It wasn't fair. How come none of them were curled up in a bathroom, crying?

I stayed in the bathroom for over an hour before I steeled myself to walk through the trailer to my bunk. I'd heard Dad move over to his bed a few minutes before, so I knew I wouldn't have to walk past him.

I stood, turning on the faucet and rinsing off my face, looking at my swollen eyes in the mirror. When I opened the door, I didn't even look at Dad, just moved directly to the table, hoisted myself up on my bed, and closed the curtains. I heard Dad sigh, but he didn't comment, which suited me fine. I'd wanted to fight with him, but now that we'd yelled, I didn't feel like it fixed anything.

I reached up and grabbed the picture of Mom and shoved it underneath the mattress pad, where I wouldn't have to see it. A few minutes later, Dad turned off the lights, plunging me into darkness.

Tears seeped through my eyelids. I propped myself up on my elbows, rubbing my eyes. I couldn't just sit here and cry all night. It was pathetic. Worse than pathetic. No wonder no one wanted me if all I did was lie around and feel sorry for myself.

Ian said I should take charge of my life, but so far I was still sitting here, letting Dad determine everything.

And meanwhile Ian sat out in the truck, chained down, unable to make decisions for himself.

I'm not sure when I knew I was going to let him go, but the decision settled over me like a warm blanket. I'd been fooling myself about running away. I didn't have the guts. But Ian could take care of himself. He could get out of here, even if I couldn't. We might both be victims of our parents' choices, but at least one of us could be free.

I waited until Dad's breaths came deep and even and ruffled with phlegm. I eased myself over to the edge of the bed, careful to move my weight gradually. That was the trouble with such an old trailer—everywhere you moved it squeaked.

Making sure not to kick the table, I extended my leg until it hit the seat below and placed my foot on the firm bench edge, hoping it would be less creaky than the middle. I lowered my weight a pound at a time, keeping my hands at the edge of the bed, my elbows locked for support. As I transferred the last of my weight, I listened.

Dad's snores were softer now but still there. I forced myself to breathe slowly and quietly as I stepped down onto the carpet.

I shifted my weight slowly again, but even so the floor let out a loud groan, like an old man easing himself into his armchair. I cringed and waited. If I wasn't supposed to do this, this was when he'd wake up. But no movement came from Dad's bed. His breaths stayed soft and even.

Kneeling, I reached out for Dad's pants, discarded on the floor. I lifted them by the belt, slowly, so they wouldn't jingle, and felt the keys in the pocket. I closed my fist around the keys so they wouldn't clink together and then pulled them out.

Setting the pants back down, I took the last two steps to the door, quick and light, with minimal squeaks from the floor. Reaching the steps, I saw the dim outline of a soda can hanging from the doorknob on a string. I looked over at the shadows on Dad's bunk. He must have put the can there so he'd hear if the door opened. But was he trying to keep Ian out or me in?

I wrapped my hand around the can and pulled it away from the door slowly, then lifted the string up and over the handle. The can made a tap as I set it on the counter. I'd have to remember to put it back.

A cold blast of air blew in as I eased the door open, and I hoped it wouldn't reach Dad under his blanket to jar him awake. Slipping out quickly, I eased the door shut again behind me.

I waited for a long, quiet moment, listening. No sounds came from inside. All the windows stayed dark. I let out my breath, watching as moonlight caught it in a steamy puff. I smiled to myself, walking around the front of the trailer, toward the truck.

A flickering orange light came from inside the cab. I stopped for a moment, planting my feet together in the gravel. At this point I could still turn back. I could quietly go back inside, and no one would have to know I was ever out here. Not Dad. Not Ian.

I could see his silhouette in the back window of the truck, hunched over in the back seat. The light sputtered and went out, then flicked on again.

My stomach squeezed with anticipation, and I knew I wasn't going back inside until I'd done what I'd come out here to do.

North Platte, Nebraska.
Hours since phone call: 4.
Distance from busted truck: 3 yards.

16

I walked quickly so I wouldn't think twice. When I got to the driver's side of the truck, I took out the keys and unlocked the rear door, pulled it open, and tucked the keys into my front pocket.

Fumes burned my nose. Ian's hands were cuffed to the floor, but he held a lighter in front of him, melting the plastic on the back of my seat. "Hey," he said.

"Hey," I said back. I stood there in the dark as Ian's flickering lighter blinked out again.

"Your dad know you're out here?"

"Nope."

Ian flicked the lighter on again.

"You trying to set yourself on fire?" I asked.

Ian shrugged. "It just melts."

"Smells awful."

"I got nothing better to do."

"Still. That can't be healthy. How'd you get that thing past my dad?"

Ian let the lighter go out again. "I have my ways. So is that what you came out here to tell me? Worried I was going to burn alive?"

"No," I said.

"What do you want, then?"

I'd come here to let him go, but now I wanted to stay with him a little while, to hold his attention. Even if Dad woke up, he probably wouldn't notice I was gone right away. Not in the dark.

I took a deep breath and climbed up onto the seat, edging along until I sat right next to Ian. Don't think, I told myself. Thoughts hurt. I wanted to feel something other than pain. I reached up, put my arms around his neck, and kissed him.

Ian didn't hesitate at all, just kissed me back hungrily. His mouth was warmer than Jamie's, and he bit at my lower lip as I pulled away. "Your dad's going to kill me," he said.

I didn't want to think about Dad. Or Jamie, or Mom. I kissed him again, pushing thoughts of them out of my mind.

I lifted my leg over Ian, resting my knees on either side of his legs and pushing my body against his.

I reached into my pocket, pulling out the keys. "Here," I said, twisting around to reach for the floor bolt. "Let me fix that."

When the chains hung free, Ian held out his handcuffs to me. I didn't want him to run away yet, so I put the keys back in my front pocket and slid his cuffed hands over my head, to rest around my neck. The chains hung down my back, dangling against my thighs as I leaned into him.

Ian pulled me closer. As our mouths met again, he reached his hands up the back of my shirt. I shivered at the brush of cold metal, but he ran the tips of his fingers across my skin in a fanning motion, and goose bumps rose on my skin.

Ian's face was only a few inches away, and he closed the distance, running his mouth along my jaw. My eyes closed in reflex, but my mind started to rush. How far did Ian expect this to go? I hadn't thought it through very well.

I pushed away a little, breathing heavy, and sat back on his knees, putting some distance between us.

The cuffs pressed into my back as he pulled me toward him again, leaning forward to meet me halfway. He kissed my collar bone, nails digging into the small of my back. His whole body pulsed, rubbing against mine.

"Do you want me to get your feet, too?" I asked, pushing back again.

"How do you know I won't run away?" he asked.

My body ached for me to shut up and keep him here. But I had to let him go. I had to. "You *will* run away," I said. "That's why I came out here. To let you go."

Ian smiled, reeling me in again like I was a fighting fish. His mouth traveled down my neck again. His hands moved up under my bra strap, massaging my skin. Even with the cuffs, his fingers were nimble enough to unhook it. He pushed his arms up under my shirt and began to lift it over my head.

My breath came sharply, and it took all my self-control to flip my leg back over him and kneel on the bench seat beside him—safely away.

"I'll get the chains," I said, reaching for his ankles to start there. At the moment, his ankles felt so much safer than his hands. I released the catch on the cuffs, then reached for his hands without looking him in the eye.

He kept his eyes on me the whole time. I could hear his breath coming fast and hard.

When I finished uncuffing him, I let the chains fall to the floor and stuck the keys back in my pocket. I expected Ian to open the car door and run into the night, but instead he knelt on the seat in front of me, pulling me up so our knees and hips touched. He ran his fingers just under the waistband of my jeans.

My heart pounded a little. Kissing him wasn't silencing my brain as much as I'd thought it would. Instead I grasped for control over my body. In my efforts not to think too hard, I hadn't considered how I was going to make him stop. Or how hard it would be to make *me* stop.

Ian's hands inched farther down my hips, and he kissed my neck more fiercely. I stiffened involuntarily.

"You should go," I said. "My dad might wake up any second." I grabbed for the door handle behind me, but it didn't open. The child lock was still on.

Ian's hands slid around my waistband to my butt. He kept kissing me, his lips making their way toward my shoulder. My body reacted instinctively, pulling away from him. The frightened little girl in me took charge over the hungry woman, dragging her over the bench seat and out the driver's-side door, escaping the heat of the cab. The damp night air was heavy. I panted to catch breaths of it.

Ian followed me out. He didn't try to grab for me again.

"What's wrong?" he asked.

"I—I'm worried about my dad, that's all. You should go. I wouldn't want him to catch you."

Ian smiled, stepping toward me. This time he kissed me on the cheek. I shivered again. The dew in the air clung to me like sweat after a breaking fever.

"Thanks," Ian said.

"Sure," I said. "You might want to stay off the freeway and away from credit cards for a while."

Ian cocked his head to the side, winking at me. "Got it."

I crossed my arms across my chest, and we looked at each other for a minute. I didn't think either of us knew what to say.

"'Night, sweetheart," Ian said, finally. Then he turned and walked confidently along the gravel road, toward the entrance to the RV park.

"'Night," I said, but only once he was too far away to hear.

For a moment I held perfectly still, feeling the echoes of his fingers against my skin. For the first time, I honestly hoped this was the last I'd see of Ian Burnham. I'd thought the rush of kissing him would make everything better, but I felt even more spun-around than before.

When Ian was out of sight, I walked carefully back to the trailer and lifted the door handle quietly. I managed to get myself in and the door shut behind me before the damn floor uttered a mighty groan under my toes.

"Hmm?" Dad said, shooting up in bed.

My hand went to my pocket, but the keys weren't there.

"I was just going to the bathroom," I said quickly, checking my back pockets, too. No keys.

What had I done with them? Were they on the floor of the truck, with the chains? No, I distinctly remembered putting them back in my pocket.

Ian. He must have taken them. But why would he do that *after* I let him go?

Dad blinked at me, hair standing up at all angles, and then looked me up and down. For a horrified moment I wondered if Ian had left marks on my neck or my face.

"You put on your shoes to go to the bathroom?" Dad asked. He raised a hand to his hair, scratching the back of his neck.

"Um, I thought I heard a noise outside," I said. "I was just checking, but I didn't see anything. It's fine. Go back to sleep."

He reached for his pants and pulled them on. "You don't check if you hear a noise. You wake me up so I can check." He rose to his feet, reaching for his shoes.

"Really, it's fine," I said. I should have made something up about my feet being cold, rather than raising Dad's suspicions. Ian probably hadn't had the chance to get far yet.

But Dad was already headed for the door. I stepped to the side.

Dad walked outside, and I heard him swear.

"Lock the trailer and stay inside," he yelled.

I heard his footsteps crunch through the gravel as he headed away.

I checked again in my pockets for the keys. Would Dad remember where he'd left them? Would he realize I must have taken them to Ian?

Movement caught my eye, over by another camper. Ian stood in the shadows. He leaned into the light, flashing a bit of metal in my direction. The keys. Maybe I'd dropped them. Was he bringing them back to me?

I stepped out the trailer door, closing it behind me and hurrying to the shadows before Dad could see I hadn't locked myself in.

Ian ducked behind a neighboring trailer, and I followed him out of Dad's sight. He grabbed me by my belt loops and pulled me into him, stuffing the keys into my back pocket. The keys jabbed my butt, and I reached to adjust them.

"Ouch," I said. "I would have taken them."

Ian didn't respond, just pulled my hips against his and kissed me hard.

My insides squirmed. I didn't want Dad to catch us, but more than that, I didn't like the way Ian was holding me, like he wouldn't let me go. The panic I'd felt in the truck crept back through me.

"Hang on," I said. "You need to get going."

Ian shook his head, wrapping his other arm around my shoulders and pushing my head into his chest. My neck tweaked, and I slammed my fists against him, trying to break away.

That's when the cold metal hit my temple. I gasped. Ian wrapped me tight against him, holding my arms so I couldn't fight.

"Don't make a sound," he said in my ear. "I don't want to hurt you, but I will if you make me."

Out of the corner of my eye I could see a gun held next to my face—Dad's handgun from the utility box on the truck. Of course Ian had stolen it. The keys were on the same ring.

"I was going to let you go," I said.

"Your old man wouldn't have," he said. "I'm not going to jail." Ian's voice sounded cold, vibrating from his chest to mine as he pulled me tighter.

Here came reality, raining down around me in cold, wet sheets. This wasn't the way I thought things would go.

Before all this was over, I might not be able to think anything at all.

Dad must have heard us, because his boots crunched closer. Ian spun me around, holding me tight to his side, the gun jabbing into my head. Dad stepped around the corner, and his whole face melted. All my doubts that he cared about me melted with it.

"Don't move, bounty man," Ian said. "Or I swear to God I will shoot her dead."

White flashes edged my vision, and I wondered if I was going to pass out. Breathe, I told myself, but my body wouldn't respond. Dad said not to point a gun at anything you don't want to shoot. Any moment now that gun might fire. Any moment now.

Dad stretched his arms into the air, pale street lighting illuminating only half his face. "I'm not armed," he said. "You can leave. Just let her go."

I stared stupidly ahead. Dad was willing to give Ian up for me. He probably had been all along.

Ian spit off to the side and pushed the barrel harder against my head. My temple gave an angry throb, and I wondered if he could kill me from pushing too hard.

"Fuck you," Ian said. "You've followed me everywhere. You're not going to let me go now."

"I swear I will," Dad said.

I could feel Ian shake his head, his chin bumping into my hair. I could feel his body shaking, his breath coming fast. The white flashes expanded, encompassing more of my vision. My own voice in my head wailed at me to breathe, but I couldn't bring my body to do it.

"You don't want to do this," Dad said. "You don't

want to add murder to the charges. You're not in that deep yet, son."

"I'm not your son," Ian said, his voice as cold as the steel against my head. "Don't follow us. She can call you when I drop her off. Until then, you don't move. If I see or hear you, I'll blow her brains out."

Chills ran over my body as he stepped back. I stumbled a bit, instinct telling me to run. Ian kept the gun on me, though, holding me to him with his arm. "Come on, sweetheart," he said. "I'm not going to hurt you if you do what I say."

I wanted to believe that Ian wasn't a murderer, that this was all for show, that he'd dumped the bullets out of the gun. But I let him pull me around the trailer, out of Dad's sight.

When we rounded a building, Ian pushed me out in front of him, making me walk before him with the gun pressing the back of my head. My vision still flashed white, but I stumbled toward the parking lot behind the park office.

I couldn't keep track of my own feet, so I tripped over a parking divider and stumbled forward. Ian watched Dad's direction, still holding the gun on me. I thought about tackling him, about wrestling the gun away from him, but couldn't even put one foot in front of the other in a straight line. Tackling him would be the action-movie thing to do. Here in the real world it was more likely to get me killed.

"Why are you doing this to me?" I asked. "I tried to help you get away."

"Yeah, but you were really bad at it."

"What about taking charge of my life, like you said? Maybe we could run off together."

"I'm not taking you with me. He'd never leave me alone then."

For the first time, I was sure that was true. Whatever had changed for Dad in the last eighteen months, he wasn't going to let me go again.

Ian ducked around another trailer, pushing me along with him. I swallowed hard. All this time I'd been flirting with him, he'd been capable of aiming a gun at my head.

"So do you do this a lot?" I whispered.

"What?"

"Armed kidnapping."

"No, sweetie," he said. "You're my first."

The way he said that made it sound dirty, and my abdomen clenched. "Please don't hurt me."

"Shut up and you'll be fine."

I kept my head down, doing as he said. A few minutes ago I'd been the one with the keys, and him the one in chains. I thought I'd been in the position of power. But maybe I never had. Maybe the gun didn't make Ian more dangerous. It just made the danger easier to see.

As we entered the parking lot, Ian stepped up to an SUV. He kept his gun pointed at me as he lifted a rock and knocked it through the window, breaking the glass. I expected an alarm to sound, but none did.

I looked around at the building, a pine tree, the streetlight, anywhere but at the gun. My whole body shook, my breath coming in short gasps.

Motion flashed in the corner of my eye, and my neck jerked toward it out of reflex. Dad came around the corner of the building, moving quietly, headed toward Ian.

I swallowed hard. Ian had told Dad not to follow or else he'd kill me. Would he follow through on his threat?

I looked around the parking lot, trying to find something to put between me and Ian. The only thing I could think of was to duck behind the car, so I leaned in that direction, looking back at Dad.

I flinched as Ian noticed my movement, glancing at me and then following my gaze in Dad's direction. His face hardened, and his gun hand jerked.

I lunged around the front of the car, hitting ground on my hands and knees and huddling down behind it.

Dad sprinted past me, shoving me out of the way. I fell flat in front of the car, asphalt gritting into my palms. I heard the thud of Dad slamming Ian against the car.

Ian's gun hand appeared over the hood, flailing, and I stayed pressed against the ground. Dad's hand wrenched the gun away from Ian and threw it to the ground. It bounced against the asphalt, landing just a few feet away from me.

I wanted to grab it, to have some way to defend myself, but I knew from practicing with Dad that I couldn't shoot straight. I'd probably shoot Dad instead of Ian. I crawled away, trying to run but not sure if I could stand. I looked back in time to see Dad elbow Ian in the face, throw him to the ground, and reach for the gun. Ian sank to the ground as Dad stood over him, pointing the gun at his head.

"Get up," Dad barked. "Let's move."

I trailed far behind as Dad walked Ian back to the truck, gun trained at the back of his neck just like Ian had done to me. When they got there, he slammed Ian against the truck door and searched him. Looking for the keys, I realized. The keys that were now in my back pocket.

Dad searched the seat, keeping the gun pointed at Ian the whole time. Ian stood with his hands behind his head, expression blank. He didn't even glance at me. The cold horror of what I'd done ripped through me. He was looking for the keys, for the way that Ian had done all of this. But it wasn't Ian who did it. It was me.

I edged toward the trailer as Dad fished around in his utility box—which was open and unlocked.

Tears seeped into my eyes, but I barely noticed them. I'd brought Ian the keys that let him get that gun. I deserved everything that came to me—losing Mom, losing Jamie. In a second Dad would be gone too. I'd almost lost him tonight. I'd almost lost myself. It was only a matter of time before Dad gave up on me. I'd be lucky if he didn't dump me with the state first thing tomorrow morning.

"Get inside," Dad shouted at me. "Stay in the trailer. I'll come get you when I figure out what we're going to do."

I ducked away, glad for the opportunity to escape. When I got back inside, I dropped the keys onto the floor. I couldn't stand to touch them. Maybe Dad would think they fell out of his pocket. Maybe he would never have to know that I had them at all. But I would know. I'd have to live with what might have happened.

I curled up on the bench next to the table, pulled my knees into my chest, and tried to stop shaking. But instead my breath came ragged, and I started to sob. The tears came fast. My whole body quaked, and I could feel the trailer trembling with it.

When I'd sat on the fence with Ian, looking at the field, I'd felt safer than I ever had with Dad. Now I understood why. It was because I knew all along he would leave me. I could predict it, like predicting a coming storm by the approaching dark clouds.

But I couldn't predict Dad. With Dad there was the possibility for hope, and in it the possibility for much more pain. I'd been using Ian every bit as much as Ian was using me—to keep Dad at arm's length, to keep him from hurting me any more than he already had.

And I'd almost gotten us both killed. Dad was right. Him, Mom, and me—we did have something in common. In the end, we all screwed over the people we loved.

I stared at the keys on the floor, glinting with gold light from the streetlamp outside. I couldn't undo what I'd done any more than Dad could take back my childhood and give me a different one. I'd betrayed Dad one too many times, and now that I'd realized that, I didn't know how to fix it. This time, maybe there wasn't a way.

North Platte, Nebraska.
Hours since the betrayal: .75.
Distance from Denver, Colorado: 265.98 miles.

17

When Dad came into the trailer to get me, I was still curled up, shaking. He stood in the doorway, back-lit by the streetlamp. My face was puffy from crying, and my nose ran. Dad didn't keep any tissues in the trailer. I wiped it on my sleeve.

"Ricki?" Dad said. "You okay?"

"Fine," I said, even though I was clearly not fine, and we both knew it.

Dad looked at me, and I knew that even in the dim light from outside I must look like a wreck. I turned my face away, but it was too late. He'd seen.

He stood quietly for a long minute, like he was trying to figure out what to say.

"I'm so glad you're safe," he said finally.

My breath shuddered. "Me too," I said.

Dad came closer, and for a moment I thought he was going to hug me, but he just sat down across the table from me and folded his hands in front of him.

"I got a mechanic to fix the brake pads. The RV attendant agreed this was an emergency, and he knew a guy he could drag out of bed. We'll get the rest done in Denver."

"This late?" I asked.

"We need this to be over with."

"Okay," I said. I still didn't move.

"I'd rather you stay here," Dad said. "But it's going to be a long drive. I wouldn't be able to get back for almost a full day."

I wished Dad would turn Ian over to the cops, but I knew he needed to get paid. I shouldn't have been here. In a hundred ways I should never have been here.

"Don't leave me alone," I said.

"Okay. But that means you're going to have to ride with us in the truck."

Dad had his spare keys in his hand. He hadn't even seen the set on the floor. I didn't know what Dad would do with me once he knew what I'd done, but the only way to tell something you don't want to say is to get on with it.

"I let him go," I said quietly.

"You what?"

"I let him go."

Dad took in a sharp breath, and I wanted to stop talking right there, but I kept going.

"I let him out of the cuffs with the keys from your pocket. That's how he got away. But I didn't think you'd wake up, and I didn't think about the gun. I didn't know what was going to happen."

I couldn't see Dad's face in the dark. "That was a damn dangerous thing to do," he said quietly. "Skips aren't safe people. I don't get why you don't understand that."

I didn't realize I was holding my breath until I had to gasp for air. "I do now," I said, thinking about the look on Ian's face as he pointed the gun at me. He'd have shot me to get away. If it came down to his freedom or my life, there was no question.

"Hell of a price to pay to figure that out," Dad said. "I could have lost you."

"I know," I said. "I'm sorry."

Dad reached across the table and put his hand on my arm. "Come on, now," Dad said. "We can talk about it later, once we're all safe."

We sat there for a minute, me sniffling, him resting

his hand on my snotty sleeve. If he noticed, he didn't show it.

"Okay," I said. "Let's just get it done."

By the time we were ready to go, Dad had Ian double chained to the floor so tight, he couldn't even sit up straight. Ian tried to catch my eye, but I didn't look at him.

I huddled in the front, not letting my back touch the seat. I couldn't be that close to Ian, even though I knew Dad had chained him good.

As we took the long drive back to Denver, the drizzle of the last few days turned to snow. Even the early-morning traffic grew thick as we merged onto I-76.

Dad kept his eyes on the road and his hands on the wheel. I wished I could sleep, but I still felt too shaky, like Ian might attack me from behind.

I reached over to switch on the radio just to distract myself. Dad caught my hand and shook his head at me. "Not now," he said. I couldn't blame him for being careful.

When we pulled up to the jail, Dad made me get out of the truck first, probably so I'd be farther away if he had any trouble with Ian after he unchained him. I stood by the trailer as Dad pulled Ian out the door, and an officer came out to meet us, swapping Dad's chains for his.

I expected Ian to say something as they took him in, but he didn't even look in my direction. He walked toward the jail with his shoulders back and his chin up. And then the doors swung closed, and he was gone.

Snowflakes dusted my hair, and I tried to pass the shaking off as a shiver. Being around Ian had been a rush, but now the rush had turned frightening.

"Let's go," Dad said, pulling open my door. I climbed into the truck, and he got in on the other side, pulling out of the parking lot and leaving Ian behind.

When Dad pulled back onto the freeway, I stared out the window. "Aren't we going to sleep?" I asked.

Dad shook his head. "I've got to go take care of the rental car first." He pulled a pack of sunflower seeds out of the glove box and offered me some. I shook my head, and he set them in his lap, tossing a few into his mouth. "Plus, the mechanic up there will have the parts to replace the rotors. The pads were a temporary fix."

I'd forgotten about the damage. "Okay," I said. That meant several more hours in the car. "Don't you need to get paid, too?"

"I'll take care of Cal tomorrow."

I folded myself against the passenger door, shivering. I finally had a story that was worth writing about. Too bad I'd never be able to bring myself to write it.

As I wrapped my arms around me, I felt as if there

213

was still someone else in the car with us. This time, though, it wasn't Ian or Stan or Alison. It was fear, hanging in the air like a ghostly presence.

"What are you going to do with me?" I asked, watching the windshield wipers flip back and forth. The pre-dawn light cast a golden sheen across the raindrops as they slipped off the glass and onto the hood.

"What do you mean?" Dad asked.

"Aren't you going to punish me?" I leaned back hard against the seat, as if pressing myself in would keep Dad from dropping me off with some foster family.

Dad sighed. "Let's start with breakfast."

He pulled into a gas station and came out with a box of doughnuts and two cups of coffee. He set the drink tray on the seat between us, and neither of us touched it until he'd pulled off at a rest stop off I-25. The sun was just rising, but all I could see of it was a golden glow through the cover of clouds and the swirl of snow.

Dad brushed the snow off the top of one of the tables, and we both sat down. The slab of cold concrete leached all the heat from my legs, and I sipped my coffee to get warm.

"I think you should know," Dad said, "that I've decided I'm not taking bounty work anymore."

"What? You can't quit your job. What will you do?"

"Cal offered me a job a while back, working as a bondsman. He's been saying for years that I'm too soft to chase skips. I never go for the big money. I bring them in, sure, but I always pick the soft ones. Always until now."

"Ian wasn't soft."

"I know. And Cal was right. I shouldn't have taken the job with you along. Ian had a record of violence. That's how they caught him—he beat up one of the guys who fenced his cars. That guy ratted him out, but they couldn't make the assault charges stick."

My cheeks burned. Reality sure was kicking me in the ass.

"Why did you take the job, then?" I asked.

"Money," Dad said. "The bounty on him is enough to get us an apartment while I get set up with Cal. I've scouted some in Denver already, set some appointments up. Of course, now some of the money will have to go to fixing this mess, but I still think we can manage."

It took a second for that to sink in. I'd been so pissed that Dad dragged me along on his bounty hunts that it hadn't even occurred to me that maybe he'd try to get out of it. And all along, he was trying to get his life to be more stable. For me.

"I don't deserve that. Not after what I did."

"Maybe not," Dad said. "I don't deserve another

chance after being such a failure of a father. Maybe we should both be glad that life doesn't always give you what you deserve."

"But you like your job. It's not fair for you to have to quit because of me."

"You're almost sixteen. In two years, you'll be off to college, and I can go back on the road if I want."

I left the college fight for another time. "What about Mom? She's still out there—and she might need help. I can't give up on her."

"There's something else I have to tell you. Something I should have told you a while back."

I looked at him. Somehow I knew this wasn't good news. "What?" I asked.

"I got a message from your mom right before I came to pick you up at Grandma's. She told me she'd taken off for California and that stuff was going so well out there, she wasn't coming back for a while. She wanted me to go pick you up—said it was my turn to be your parent."

His turn. Like I was a part-time job and she was asking to switch shifts.

So that's why he refused to look for her. It wasn't about her constitutional rights at all. He already knew she didn't want me. "Why didn't you tell me?"

"I've been trying to get hold of her since," Dad said.

"I figured if I could reach her, I could change her mind. She called me on a pay phone the first time, so I had a hard time tracking her down. I didn't want to tell you that she wasn't coming back. Not unless I had to."

"You lied. You told me you weren't looking for her."

"I know. I didn't want you to get your hopes up. So I made the phone calls when you were at the library. You didn't make it easy, though, always going on about how she might have gotten kidnapped."

I rubbed the back of my neck, trying to process this.

Little snowflakes melted on my cheeks. I probably should have cried then, but I was still running on the shock of last night. Six hours of sleep in two full days meant the dial on my emotions was stuck on low. "So did you find her?"

Dad reached into his breast pocket and pulled out one of his business cards and handed it to me. "I made some calls," he said. "Had a PI friend who owed me a favor. He called me last night with this number."

I looked down at the card, and scrawled in Dad's handwriting was a ten-digit phone number. "She's staying with her friend Denis. We tracked them down through that dating website she was on."

"I know about him," I said. "I found a bunch of messages she sent him before she disappeared. He lives in San Diego."

Dad took a long swig of his coffee. "Good work."

"Did you call her yet?"

"No. I've been trying to decide what to say. But maybe I haven't called because it's your call to make."

"You should have told me," I said. "I deserved to know about the message."

"You're probably right," Dad said. "But I really thought she'd change her mind and you'd never have to know."

"So why are you telling me now?"

Dad sighed. "Because I don't know what else to do. I'm trying, Ricki, but I still don't know what the hell I'm doing."

That confession startled me even more than the news that he'd heard from Mom. I knew Dad didn't know what he was doing, but for the first time I realized that he was aware of it.

"I'm kind of bad at being your daughter, too," I said. "So I guess we're even."

"That's a hell of a thing to be even at. Maybe we can work on it."

I turned the business card over in my hand. I wanted to believe Mom would hear my voice and realize she'd made a terrible mistake. But Dad was already planning to get an apartment in Denver, to fix things up so I could stay with him.

I needed to call Mom now. This couldn't wait. "Can I use your phone?"

Dad handed me the cell phone. "You can use it right now if you want."

I pinched the card between my fingers, as if by holding on to the card I could make Mom answer the phone, make us be okay.

I stood up from the table. I didn't want him listening in. Dad looked up at me as I walked away, leaving footprints in the snow. "Ricki," he said, "I know I haven't been a model father, but I won't walk out on you. You have my word on that."

I wasn't sure I could bring myself to believe that. I didn't deserve that kind of a promise, not after what I'd done. But maybe Dad was right. Life didn't always give us the things we deserved. Sometimes that sucked, but sometimes it was a lucky thing.

"Thanks," I said. I walked around the far side of the restrooms and huddled under the eaves. I punched the numbers from the card into the phone, listening to the ring on the other end.

Rest stop outside Denver, Colorado.
Seconds into phone call: 3.
Distance from Dad: 10 yards.

18

"Hello?" Mom said. Hearing her voice took me so much by surprise that I thought I'd pee my pants.

"Mommy? Mom?"

"Ricki baby?" Mom said. "Where'd you get this number?"

Not *Are you okay?* Not *How have you been?* Not *I am so sorry. Where'd you get this number?* The relief I'd felt at hearing Mom's voice hardened.

"Dad found it," I said. "What happened? Where have you been?"

"Oh, honey, things have been so crazy. I'm sorry. I should have called, but I knew you'd be safe with Grandma and that your dad would take care of you."

"It's been a month, Mom. Do you realize it's been a month?"

"I know, sweetie. I was going to call tomorrow. I promise I was. Just as soon as things calmed down."

"Right," I said. "Well, Dad said you told him you weren't coming back. That it was his turn to take care of me."

"Have you been staying at his place?" she asked. "Is he feeding you okay?"

She'd dodged the question. "He's driving me around in his travel trailer chasing after fugitives. It's pretty awful, actually."

"Oh, baby, I'm so sorry. I'd have come home if I knew."

"If you were going to come home, why did you tell Dad you didn't want me anymore?" My voice was edging on hysterical, but I couldn't help it.

Mom's voice sharpened a bit. "Don't be like that."

"What do you mean, don't be like that? *You* walked out on *me*."

"That's not fair, honey."

I didn't want to fight now. We could fight later, once we had things all sorted out. The important thing now was to get us back together.

"Dad can drive me to where you are," I said. "So you won't have to come get me."

Mom was quiet for a moment. "Aw, honey . . . honey, I'd love to, but I can't right now."

"What do you mean, you can't? I said Dad would bring me. You don't even have to do anything."

"You remember Denis? The man I met online? Well, I'm staying at his place, and it's small, only one bedroom. We'd be living on top of each other, sweetie, and Denis and I are still figuring out our relationship. Besides, it wouldn't be fair to you, living in a place like this."

"Then come home, Mom."

"I'm sorry, honey. But things with Denis are going so well. And you know what a hard time I've had finding a decent guy. I can't walk out on him when things are finally starting to work out for me. You understand?"

I understood. I'd heard her. Her needs came first, my needs came second, and I hated myself for being surprised.

"That's fine, Mom," I said. "Look, I've got to go."

"I'll call you soon, okay? See if Dad will take you back to Grandma's. It's not fair for you to have to live in a trailer like that."

"Dad's getting an apartment in Denver," I said. "I'm going to stay there with him." At the moment that felt worlds better than living in an apartment with her and *Denis*, the man she'd known a month whose needs took precedence over mine.

"That's good, honey. It's only for a little while. And

then we'll get set up with a bigger place, and I'll send for you."

That was the sort of thing you told a three-year-old who wanted a cookie you knew she'd forget about. In a little while. Bullshit.

"Sure, Mom," I said.

She didn't catch my sarcasm.

"Okay. You take care of yourself."

"Right. Bye." When I hung up, I realized I hadn't even told her that I loved her.

I sat there for a few minutes, hugging my arms to my chest. A breeze blew by, raising goose bumps on my skin.

Mom wasn't hurt. She just didn't want me. And I ought to have felt awful about that, to have hated her for it. But my chest felt empty, as if my body was running on fumes—no emotion left.

There was only Dad now. He wasn't perfect, but at least he was trying. That's what he'd been telling me all along.

When I came back, Dad was sitting in the cab of the truck, out of the snow. Who ate doughnuts in the snow, anyway? We were both a couple of crazy people.

When I climbed into the cab beside him, he handed me a doughnut. "So," Dad asked, "you okay?"

The seat squeaked as I settled onto it. "I don't know," I said.

"You need a ride to California?"

"No," I said.

He was quiet for a moment. We both knew what that meant.

"She all right?"

"She doesn't want me."

"Ricki—"

"No, it's true. It's really stupid, but it's true."

"So are you going to stay with me?"

"Why would you want me to do that?"

"Maybe so we can both have that second chance we were talking about."

I wrapped my arms around my waist, squeezing tight. We were never going to get through this if I couldn't bring myself to ask those unaskable questions.

"What if you find something you'd rather be doing than living with me?" I asked. "What happens the day I come home and you've gone off chasing some bounty and left me a note?" My insides trembled just thinking about it.

Dad paused for a moment. "I won't do that."

"What's changed?"

"What's changed is you need me."

"Maybe I always needed you."

"Maybe I didn't understand that until now. And I don't deserve forgiveness for that, but I am sorry. You have my word, though. I won't walk away. I'll give you a place to stay for as long as you need. That's a promise."

I leaned back, looking up at the torn cloth ceiling. I didn't want to believe him. Believing him would set me up to be hurt again. But running away would turn me into someone I didn't want to be—into a skip, even if I never broke the law. Taking that risk might be the only way to build a life that was real.

"Won't be so bad, being in Denver. When we find a place, we can get you into a real school. We can even head back to Utah now and again, so you can see your friends."

I stared at him. He still didn't act much like a dad. And there was no guarantee that he wouldn't dump me off somewhere as soon as he realized I wasn't going to morph into some ideal daughter, even if I wanted to. But if I didn't believe him now, I'd never know if what he said might have been true. I'd never know if he was ready to stick around. I'd have to run off, and where would that land me? I'd be like Ian—always running.

"I'm still not sure how to trust you," I said.

Dad actually laughed. "I'm not sure how to trust you either, after the last few days. I imagine that comes with time. You try to stay out of trouble, and I'll try not to get you into any for a change."

"Okay," I said. "But you better let me help you look

for an apartment," I said. "Because I'm not going to live in some dump."

Dad laughed again, and I couldn't help but smile myself. I'm not sure which one of us moved first, but we both leaned across the bench seat, and he wrapped his arms around my shoulders, squeezing. Our jackets squished together, and my face pressed against the melted snow on his shoulder.

"You won't regret this, Ricki," he said into my hair.

And for the first time, I really believed he was right.

ACKNOWLEDGMENTS

Thanks to Eddie, agent extraordinaire, for the sharp and diligent work on this book and, most especially, for putting up with my many neuroses. In addition, thanks are due to the whole team at JABberwocky—the best agents in the business.

Thanks also to Christy and the team at Henry Holt for helping to shape this book into what it is now.

In addition, thanks to the many people who read my early drafts and offered feedback: the Rats with Swords—Eric, Dan, Brandon, Emily, Isaac, Karla, Rachel, and Ben. Also the wonderful people of the BYU MA program, especially Chris and the best writing class ever—James, Erin, Ryan, Carol, Tessa, Shayne, and Lesley—who read the book earliest of all and were still encouraging. And to my beta readers, Sandra and Jillena.

And thanks, most recently, to the Seizure Ninjas—Heidi, Cavan, Alex, and Lee Ann—for their support over the last few years.

Special thanks are due to Kristy, who never lost enthusiasm for my work, despite having read more undeveloped drafts than anyone. Without her excellent feedback, all my books would be much, much worse. Also to Brandon, for telling me I could do this, and then teaching me how. His continued support has been too critical to describe in brief.

Thanks to Big Mike, for the use of his name. And to Bob Burton, for writing the best manual on bounty hunting around.

And last of all, thanks to my husband, Drew, without whom I would never have thought to write about bounty hunting in the first place. Thanks for the hours of brainstorming, the feedback on multiple drafts, and, most important, for believing in me even when I'd lost faith in myself. Working with you is an honor; living with you is a celebration. I love you.